DATE DUE

JUL 7 1987	JUN 06 1999	
DEC 21 1988	7/01	
JUL 10 1991	MAY 19 2001	
JUN 02 1992		
AUG 28 1992		
AUG 27 1992		
NOV 02 1992		
DEC 13 1992		
MAY 06 1993		
JUN 16 1993		
OCT 16 1993		
DEC 17 1998		

HIGHSMITH 45-220

HEREMAKHONON

A Novel

HEREMAKHONON

A Novel

By Maryse Condé

TRANSLATED FROM THE FRENCH
BY
RICHARD PHILCOX

AN ORIGINAL BY THREE CONTINENTS PRESS, INC.

© Maryse Condé 1982

First English Language Edition

Three Continents Press
1346 Connecticut Avenue N.W.
Washington, D.C. 20036

ISBN: 0-89410-232-X
         0-89410-233-8 (pbk)

LC No: 81-51667

Cover Design by Tom Gladden

Hérémakhonon was originally published in French by Union Générale in 1976 (Paris).

To Richard

*Je crois volontiers les histoires dont
les témoins se font égorger.*
                                    Pascal

Heremakhonon

One

Honestly! You'd think I'm going because it is the in thing to do. Africa is very much the thing to do lately. Europeans and a good many others are writing volumes on the subject. Arts and crafts centers are opening all over the Left Bank. Blondes are dying their lips with henna and running to the open market on the rue Mouffetard for their peppers and okra.

Well, I'm not! Seven hours in a DC-10. On my left, an African desperately trying to make small talk. Behind me, a French couple as average as they come. Why am I doing this? At the moment, everything is a mess, and this whole idea seems absurd. I can see them now. My mother, sighing as usual. My father pinching his thin lips. (Not all blacks have protruding lips.)

"She's insane! So headstrong! All those brains and nothing but foolish ideas."

Foolish? Maybe he's right for once.

"Purpose of visit?"

The police officer really hits the nail on the head. His uniform—it could only be described as laughable. If ever one can say that of a policeman's uniform. The thin, nervous type. Somewhat distinguished. Surely from that part of the coast that produced my father's ancestors. He too was somewhat on edge and somewhat handsome. He reminded me of that Mandingo marabout I had seen in my history book when I was seven. And not from the South either, but from Dahomey or Nigeria, men who had paid their fair share to what they called the New World. The New World? All that for a few Venetian glass beads, a few rolls of red cotton, a portable organ for Agadja and a carriage for Tegbessu. All that for so little!

Purpose of visit? No, I'm not a trader. Not a missionary. Not even a tourist. Well, perhaps a tourist, but one of a new breed, searching out herself, not landscapes.

The hotel keeper is straight out of a third rate movie. He must have elbowed his way through Indochina, Algeria and wherever else they butchered the sub-species.

"Where you from?"

The French, and consequently everyone else, have always ignored Guadeloupe in favor of Martinique. The Martinique women are said to have a higher proportion of mixed blood. Hence they are considered more beautiful. A whole lot of good that did them. They merely provided more bastards for the Empire and more fodder for the slaughter. Why am I here? They were right to sneer. Not my mother, she never sneers. She sighs:

"We never really understood her."

That's it! Misunderstandings all the way. Tons of them, right up to the first goodbye. They, standing behind the glass doors at the airport. Me, climbing the gangway with wobbly legs and misty eyes. Beside me, a plump woman with a burst of flamingo flowers in her arms and her soft voice saying:

"Don't cry, little one. You'll be back for the holidays."

The holidays? Nine years since I have not been back, as they say. Nine years since I have seen the flamingo flowers, the bougainvillea, the poinsettias, the flame trees. Musn't get sentimental. No, not that. There's been too much of that, rivers of sentiment.

"Welcome to Africa."

Where did *he* spring from? He too is tall and thin, a bit like a bean pole in his pale green boubou.

"Consider yourself home."

With one word, he has wiped out three centuries and a half. Instead of riding the new coach and practicing scales, Tegbessu and Agadja have positioned their men at strategic points. They are driving the whites back into the sea. It is glowing red with blood. The slave ships in Nantes and Liverpool have been set afire. They have served their purpose. But let's face it. This one is not much to look at. The collar of his boubou is frayed. One would never believe that he holds an *agrégré d'histoire,* this director of the national institute to which I was insane enough to hire my services. My father the Mandingo marabout used to say that appearances were everything. *For form's sake.* How many times we heard that. Even on the beach we were not allowed to walk barefoot, to feel the warm sand. We were hardly out of the water when our maid, Mabo Julie, was running toward us with our sandals in her hands. Our naked toes were like crabs barred from their natural habitat.

"I would like to give you a more appropriate welcome, but we are going through a period of austerity."

Why does he smile so much? True, I expected something else. Didn't rumor have it that they had rushed to take over the luxurious villas deserted by the whites? Wasn't that the reason why they grabbed their independence, to get the white man's villa and the white man's woman? Everybody knows the white woman is the black man's obsession. Not *this* black man.

"This is my wife, Oumou Hawa."

The black gazelle extolled by the poet. Pregnant, not that it mars her beauty. Nothing could.

The table is set for two. They're right, a woman's place is in the kitchen. One could always begin with the classic confession, lonely hearts style. For example: It was pointless, an affair that dragged on and on. An affair and nothing but. She knew in her heart that she wanted a husband, children, a car, all the good things in life . . . Well, she got a car alright.

Aida and Jalla had posed for *their* pictures in white veil and tiara. Jean-Michel had laughed his head off:

"What a *picture* your sisters make! You'll just have to take me to the West Indies."

Aida had married a doctor, the son of a doctor friend of the marabout. A success story. Jalla had deviated somewhat. She had married a lawyer, the son of a former mechanic. The father-in-law was a union leader whose sudden death had plunged the movement into mourning. They had even named a cultural center after him. It sure needed some local celebrity to counterbalance Belain d'Esnambuc and all the others. The niggers had to build their own Pantheon of famous men, didn't they? The Mandingo marabout was proud of his ancestors and he was right. This tastes good, what is it?

"Chicken with groundnuts."

Even so, it's nice to be welcomed by this stranger. My boss. Three centuries and a half wiped out.

The whites are coming! The whites are coming!

It seems they took them for ghosts. Ancestors reincarnated. Curdled milk was splashed in front of them as an act of propitiation. Curdled milk against cannon balls. Not surprising they had not gone very far.

Right now, Oumou Hawa is bringing in oranges.

"Veronica liked your chicken and groundnuts."

She smiles. What the hell am I doing here? I need to be alone. Put my thoughts in order, as they say. Start all over again from the beginning. But where did it all begin? You might say, of course, it was the doll's christening party. Do they have doll parties in other lands? The doll all wrapped in lace, black nannies all dressed up, children aping adults. Yes, I suppose you might say that was the beginning. Dr. Rozier, yet another of the marabout's friends, had saved Mme de Roseval from certain death. A black doctor saving the life of an upper class mulatto! All the others had written her off. They had even advised against sending her to France. She would not last the journey. But Rozier, ex-resident doctor from the Paris hospitals, went to work with his lancet and the lady recovered. Hence, the relations built on deep gratitude. Her grandchildren had condescended to attend the doll's christening. But that's a false start. It must have started well before that. The beginning was lost in the mists of time.

De Roseval. The name sparkled on the bottles: of rum, liqueur, and punch, below the traditional Arawak, scarfaced and bedecked in feathers. The family lived a few miles from town on the road to Fonds de Terre. And the tourists doing Island Tour No. 5—north, northeast, Pointe du Nègre, Ajoupa-Bouillon and the magnificent Hotel de l'Escale—were driven past the Roseval mansion at Hauteurs Sainte-Marie. Those who, like the Mandingo marabout, knew their colonial history by heart, would laugh. The mansion was a fake, a mere copy of the Marins de St Sorlins mansion which had stood a few miles higher up only to be brought down in a slave uprising. You can check it at the public library if you're interested. It happened just before 1789 when our ancestors had had enough. The light-skinned Rosevals claimed descendance from the Marins de St Sorlins. One of them had even attempted to prove it. All the whites rose up against him. Pretentious bastard.

Anyway, this would be a likely start. For years I remained bowled over that he noticed me. Me, Veronica, full of anti-grace. My sisters in white muslin dresses, their white socks pulled up tight over their chocolate calves playing Ravel's *Pavane pour une infante défunte.* I was always sulking in a corner and yet it was me. This light-skinned mulatto with green eyes and the complexion of a young Oriental prince. (A fifteen year old's comparisons are always silly.) Since then, I have not gotten over my fascination for light colored eyes. Perhaps I already had it. Very likely.

"Would you care for a cup of *chaudo.*"

Chaudo is our national drink, after the rum punch, of course. It flows white, thick and sickeningly sweet at christenings, weddings and first communions. It smells of orange blossoms, but at least it does not make one drunk. I stammered a bit when he said this incredible thing:

"I'm bored stiff . . . Let's beat it."

Beat it? Where? Rafale, the dog, is standing guard at the door and one hundred pairs of eyes are watching.

"Follow me."

Possibly this makes a beginning. Why do I feel like telling it to the bean pole, my boss, in his frayed boubou? Is it affection? Or rather like choosing a perfect stranger to tell one's troubles to? I'm sobbing it all out to this blonde woman on the subway platform of the Vincennes-Neuilly line. Or in the bar on the rue Durantin while this bald man who's obviously been through it all too is consoling me. A sudden din startles me. The bean pole smiles:

"It's Saturday."

African drums. Who has not heard of them? They say the white missionaries used to listen, panting and making the sign of the cross under their mosquito nets: Satan's worshippers. How naive can you be! For me, there's nothing very extraordinary about drums. These are hardly any different from our own *massa kon* at carnival time. Hardly any different from the *gros ka* at village fairs with which the blacks express their lust for life with the same guts they use for living. Put them in irons, brand them with red hot tongs, cart them off to the cotton and cane fields and what do you get? Jazz with the beguine and calypso thrown in as a bonus. These are the drums who make American tourists shiver to the chicken blood splattering a voodoo ceremony: "Papa Legba, open up the way! What are you waiting for? It's time!"

The Mandingo marabout used to say such dances should be

forbidden. "If they did not dance, they would already be free." It was a vicious circle. They danced to forget. And since they forgot, all they ever felt like doing was dancing.

It was his tone of voice that was remarkable, the chill of his contempt. *He,* of course, was free. Free no longer to walk on the bare soles of his feet. Free to stick his neck in a white bow tie. Free to welcome his Sunday guests with a pompous "Eloise, you're *divine!*" Divine niggers! Can you dig it! His freedom was an iron weight encircling his feet and ours. And now, this young mulatto with his "I'm bored stiff. Let's beat it!"

It wasn't the name I fell for, I swear. As far as that goes, I had nothing to be jealous of. The name of the Mandingo marabout was not splashed over rum bottles, but it was on the title pages of literary magazines. It was the signature at the end of speeches for the Floral Contest and similar ceremonies. It was engraved on the black plate on the door to our house: MR. MERCIER, SOLICITOR. So it's no use following that trail. It wasn't his color either. Jean-Marie de Roseval was quite simply good looking. He still is. And will be for some time if drink does not do him in. Divine justice, one might say, as his family got rich by producing liquors and spirits. The booze is destroying him. Not rum. That's for niggers. *He* puts back whiskey and gin. We saw each other again five years ago. During a stopover in Paris, he asked me to dinner and I was foolish enough to accept.

"You're the only girl I've ever really loved."

No, let's not get sentimental.

Wasn't his color, I swear. That's what they all said because, naturally, they could not think of anything else. No, it was his freedom. The bean pole smiles. He has a lovely smile, rounded teeth, very white. Careful! Beware of clichés: the nigger with flashing white teeth. All the same, his teeth are very white.

"I have to go. To a meeting. You'll find out that, in this country, there are always meetings. I shall leave you in the hands of one of your future students, Birame III."

"Why III?"

He smiles again.

"Because there are three of them with the same name in the same class from the same village."

Birame III is a younger version of the bean pole. A white boubou, also frayed and very dirty. His nails! It's obvious he does not have a Mabo Julie to inspect all the different parts of his body. He suggests we visit the town. Don't they know I don't care a damn for their town? I'm not an ordinary tourist. I don't care a damn for the women lined up at the well with their babies on their backs. I don't care a damn for the men sleeping in folding chairs in front of their mud huts! I'm not trying to get out of my element. The dubious thrill of exoticism . . .

"Even so, what living conditions!"

Poverty and filth are nothing new to me. I've been looking at them ever since I was born, gazing through the half open window of my father's car. They used to thrive in their huts built out of cardboard boxes. We didn't have dried mud at home. The children would come running after the Peugeot with their oversized tattered coats, their sex hanging out front. The old women would puff on their pipes and shake their heads. I am looking . . . What am I looking for in this land of Africa?

"How do you like our town?"

I don't care a damn, dear little Birame III. I haven't come here to count the number of buildings erected since independence. I'd better tell him, there have been enough misunderstandings.

"What do you mean you're not involved in politics. It's not possible."

I'm afraid it is. You get involved despite everything. The Mandingo marabout used to accuse me of playing the left-wing intellectual. Intellectual, OK; but left-wing? And all because I would not have my picture taken with a white veil and tiara in front of the cathedral? I turned my nose up at our trips to France where the children would be taken to hear the aria from Lakmé or gaze at the Victory of Samothrace and the Venus de Milo minus the arms.

"What wonderful things the whites have accomplished!"

"What about us?"

"What about us? They let us stand back and admire. Isn't that enough?"

Left-wing intellectual. Whore. These were the names a father calls his daughter. Anyway, I'm not the first in the family. His half-sister, Paula, was an easy lay. Lebanese, Syrians, French sailors from the *Jeanne,* they all laid her. It was only the niggers she would not have because they wanted it for free. To make a long story short, a down-and-out white, determined to finish his days under the Caribbean sun, married her on his death bed. The priest had threatened to withdraw the last rites. She was left the lovely French name of Delahaye and enough to build a hotel-restaurant on the public square at Sainte Anne. They never mentioned her name. Black-out. The fuss when they found out I used to meet Jean-Marie in her house! Why did she do it? Not out of vice or perversion as they believed. She just thought it would do me good. She would relive her life through me, but an improved version. Instead of a balding, wheezing white with a limp prick, I'd have myself a rich young mulatto with a permanent hard on. Aunt Paula came to Paris. She was wealthy. Jean-Michel and I took her out. She was wearing an enormous necklace and earrings the size of avocados. Real gold! Jean-Michel was splitting his sides.

"Know who she looks like?"

Mahalia Jackson, streetwalking before she became a gospel singer. We're all related. All off the same boat. We all look alike. Another uproar, this time whistles, sirens, cars flashing past.

"The President's motorcade . . . "

What's Birame III laughing about?

"You know what the president calls himself? Mwalimwana . . ."

It means our Father.

Birame III, Birame III, it's none of my business. I told you. And after all, I like the sound of Mwalimwana.

The presidential cavalcade has caused a traffic jam and the police are blowing on their whistles as hard as they can. What a lot of policemen in this place. The pavements are thick with them. Better than prostitutes, perhaps. No blennorrage or syphilis.

"Look Mademoiselle!"

What does he want me to look at now? How old can he be? Sixteen, seventeen at most. Exactly my age when I used to slip out at night. Obviously if you've eaten your fill since childhood, you've plenty of time to think of love and nothing else. Racine wrote his plays for the King and his court. What childhood did *he* have? I can guess. My father is an errand boy. My mother is his second wife. She has already been married once and divorced. From this first marriage, she had four children. Only one survived and is living with his father. I have half-brothers from my father's first wife. When I was two, my mother quarrelled with my father and took me back to the grandmother who had brought her up. My father sent for me immediately. I stayed three years with him, then went home to my mother. One day, father's nephew, an accountant who was raised with him by the elder brother, came and said: "Hand over the child!" He's the one who made me go to school. Every day I have to fight for my share of rice. And nobody buys me any clothes. I'm all alone and miserable.

What are we doing in this broken down car? My boss is really not up to par. A Skoda. Is this all he can afford for a car? Why hasn't he got a Mercedes from the President's motorcade? He's got an aggregation for God's sake. There can't be that many in this country. The Mandingo marabout was fond of saying that education is the key. That's why we had to sweat through all kinds of private lessons. We had to be first in everything. I must admit that, for me, it was not difficult.

"She's got the brains! If she wanted . . . "

I had only one blind spot: music. I couldn't play an instrument to save my life. My great uncles, the jazzmen, must have been furious. Mlle Thermopyle, our teacher, an old spinster with a black straw hat, was so disheartened:

"You're in the key of A. A."

How grateful I was for that blind spot. They would leave me alone when there was a reception. I would not, like Aida or Jalla, be called upon to play a piece from the piano primer. I escaped having to kiss Bishop Duchapuis' ring when he visited the diocese, a guest of honor at the cultural soirées.

"Mademoiselle, history will pass judgment for all that blood!"

Birame III, what are you talking about? Do you know what you're saying? Don't you know that history never bothered about niggers? It's been proven they weren't worth the fuss. They had no part in building the Golden Gate Bridge or the Eiffel Tower. Instead of praying at Notre Dame or Westminster Abbey, they knelt before a piece of wood, bowed down to a snake. A *snake,* can you imagine?

The very same that tempted Eve! And they would make it into an ancestor or god. It's with the lash they had to be civilized, given not just a history they needn't be ashamed of, but a *history,* period! You might think that everybody has a history. Well, no. These people had none. But I refused to believe it. I insisted:

"But before?"

Before the family saga. The great grandfather or great great grandfather who had bought his freedom with a lot of patience and hard work . . .

"Eia for the royal cailcedra . . . "

His freedom and a plot of land. Set up house with Florimonde, an honest, hardworking negress whose children had, one by one, climbed the rungs of the social ladder. Up from slavery. Good old Booker T.

"Before!"

Faces fell and lost their expression of pride.

"We were in Africa."

I know, I know. What were we doing there? We must have lived, *somehow.* Eaten, slept, raised children? Was it so savage and horrible that it is better forgotten? Who can tell me? No one. Because nobody knows and everyone takes for granted what they've been told. Birame III, that's mainly why I'm here. To try and find out what was before.

The bean pole smiles. I'm beginning to like his smile. He has asked me to call him Saliou. That makes me feel good. Less than twenty-four hours in this country and already a friend. Somebody to talk to. He is making mint tea while his eldest son sits on his left knee. His second son is sleeping on his mother's back while she pounds in the yard. Not a word. They know how to treat women here. Pregnant, one month to go, and she's pounding. Not like my mother who always had something wrong. The sugar cane in flower always gave her a kind of hay-fever. Can you imagine it! The sugar cane in flower! It's as if the sight of coal made a miner's daughter sick. After all, where would we be if Christopher Columbus hadn't crossed the Atlantic with his ship's hold full of sugar cane plants taken from the Moslems in Cyprus? We ought to make it our emblem, our standard. If man is a (thinking) reed, the West Indian is a stalk of sugar cane.

Mother would get such sneezing fits. And the marabout would sigh.

"Mother is so fragile."

My mother's family was not discussed often either. I knew that grandmother Bonne Maman (she died when I was six), whose cold, sticky cheek I can still feel, was the daughter, illegitimate of course, of a *bakra* by the name of Sainte-Croix de la Ronseraie. We used to see the Sainte-Croix de la Ronseraie in the center aisle of the cathedral on Sundays. They didn't bother giving us a look. I'm sure they didn't know a drop of their grandfather's sperm had started our family line. We, on the other hand, had mounted and embalmed it. It was responsible for my mother's relatively light skin and Aida's straight nose. Its long-lasting quality kept us from being as black as coal. We were *negresses-rouges*.

"What a lovely dilly skin," my mother used to say, kissing me. Despite everything, she did kiss me. Mid-July, after prize-giving, when I had walked off with all of the possible prizes.

"All those brains. If she wanted to . . . "

The Mandingo marabout would also kiss me. Come on now.

They weren't ogres.

Simply, "We can't understand her."

Now Saliou, what were you saying? I have always been very bad at listening to others.

"You have to adapt your teaching . . . "

Is that all? Kwame Nkrumah? I've nothing against him. Simply I never thought he deserved the name of philosopher. I'm not one to put people down. I'll delve into Consciencism, his key concept. I'll lecture on it. I've been brought up so thoroughly on intolerance that I'm remarkably tolerant. So there'll be no more Spinoza, Rousseau, Bergson in my philosophy classes? Good. They're not essential. No, they hardly talked about my mother's family. Bonne Maman it seems was a widow. She wore two wedding rings on her left hand. My mother was an only daughter. Which saved us, unlike the Roziers, from having unkempt aunts and uncles coming down from their native Grands-Fonds once a year and obliging us to play host.

We had a cousin, though. Cousin Seraphin. Sometimes he used to come for Sunday lunch with his wife, cousin Charlotte. At the end of the meal he used to say: "Thank you cousin Marthe. I've eaten my fill."

And he would smile at me across the table. Did he know what they said behind his back?

"Would you like to go to a reception at the President's palace?"

Oh no Saliou! I haven't crossed the oceans for that. I've had my fill of receptions at the Prefecture or the President's palace, it's all the same. Group photos on the front page of the newspapers, in the gossip columns. Tonight I'll go back to my hotel, lay my head on my pillow and sleep. And perhaps he won't haunt my dreams. Since I've been in Africa he has left me in peace. Each morning he would sweep the rue de l'Université. He would look at Jean-Michel and me, no hatred, no anger, no intolerance, no amazement. Some of them call out as you go by.

"Where are you from, Sister?"

He didn't say anything. Just looked. Me and my architect with his long hair and rust-colored velvet suit. The first time I dreamed of him I couldn't get over it. Dream of a street cleaner!

"Perhaps you want him to lay you . . . He's good-looking."

Jean-Michel's explanations were always along these lines. Like all Europeans he had heard of Freud and given him a personal touch. But when I saw him coming back night after night I started to get worried.

"Veronica, what have you come to do here?"

At long last! Saliou hadn't wasted time asking the key question. Only he is less of a stranger than the blonde woman on the Vincennes-Neuilly line or the bald man in the bar on the rue Durantin. All that's missing is the psychiatrist's couch. The small boy on his knee is crying for some unknown reason. In the yard, the thud of Oumar Hawa's pestle. How to confide with such noise? Despite the kindness in his eyes. Let's try. I'm concentrating. I've already mentioned the doll's christening. Where have I already talked about that? . . . We're out in the street.

La Pointe is a small town that can hardly attract visitors for it consisted mainly of warehouses. Barrels of salted meat, crates of cod, in salt too, oil and gasoline drums, barrels of rum and sugar (again!) went up for sale under the overheated corrugated iron roofs. The whites had built their homes several miles higher up on the hill. In time the town had split up into three zones: the old district around the port with its warehouses and wide, deserted streets lined with ancient sandbox trees; the upper town at the foot of the Morne Salée with its balconied houses, the homes of La Pointe's illustrious families, and the lower town or, in modern terms, shantytown. They tell me that a new town was built recently next to the one I just described, modeled on the council flats in the vicinity of Paris. Progress is knocking on our door! But I haven't seen this new town. It's nine years since I've been back. If I went back they would all be at the airport. The Mandingo marabout like the others. Dirty linen is kept in the family. I'm meeting my daughter. And, in a way, I'm paying homage through the family to the whole Race. Booker T. would not have hesitated to kiss me on both cheeks. And I would have a place in *Ebony*.

The little boy is crying louder. Oumou Hawa takes him in her arms and Saliou and I are left face to face. Saliou, whom I didn't know the day before yesterday and who says I'm his sister. No, Saliou, I can't. Something says no.

Night has fallen. The bats are shrieking in the cotton trees. Women are dancing wildly, legs wide apart. What's uppermost in their minds? Tomorrow's rice and don't let my co-wives in their jealousy unleash their marabouts on me.

A marabout, that's what I need. Western medicine has no effect.

He sits down cross-legged on the ground. He draws in the sand and look serious. "Big man, big business."

Try, try. I'll pay anything to recover. A marabout or a medium. I've already been to see one medium. I'm not ashamed of saying so, because I was not being driven by that deep tribal instinct which we have in us, black and thick as blood. No, I was just seventeen and madly in love. Aunt Paula put her hand in mine and steamrolled her buttocks under her patterned dress.

"It was thanks to her that Delahaye ended up marrying me. She worked on it and worked on it."

Me and marriage! I had no intention of sitting in the de Roseval's pew between Claire-André and Alexandra, now my sisters-in-law.

The island lived to some extent with all eyes focused on the de Rosevals. Which of the two sisters was the most beautiful? O, the prestige of the mulatto! It would be a fairytale wedding. All the little black girls would see themselves in my shoes, a black marrying a mulatto. But, I swear, all I wanted was to have it last a lifetime, wedding ring or not.

The dormeuse had large frog's eyes and a deep wheezing voice. She nodded her head in the candlelight.

"It won't be easy."

For months I poured into my bath the stinking contents of a bottle. Afterwards I soaked myself in Bourjois perfume (I'm sorry, that's all I used at the time). Mabo Julie was surprised. And my mother:

"She's becoming very coquette."

Birame III slips into the room. They have a silent way of moving. Beware of clichés! No. That's how they move. He sits down in a chair facing me, beside Saliou. I think they are related after all. This young man is reading. And what is he reading? *Principles of Marxism-Leninism* in the Moscow foreign-language edition. I think that's tremendous. Actually taking pleasure in reading such a book at his age. But perhaps it's the only age when it is a pleasure. Because you can still believe in it. The bean pole is talking to me. Or rather Saliou, my brother.

"I've asked Birame III to teach you Mande."

That's the least I can do, me the daughter of a marabout. So it was from here, right here where we came from. I might have been called Mariama or Salamata and worn my hair in corn rows. I could have vibrated to the word of the griot. Listen, listen children of the black country. I'm going to speak of Malikoma. Malikoma, son of Sirriman, son of Fania, son of . . . up to the very beginning. May peace be with you.

Instead, I have in my family tree a white man's sperm gone astray in some black woman's womb. It didn't seem to disgust the sailors on the slave ships and they had made a number of them pregnant by the time they reached land. In fact, that's how it all began.

O, the prestige of the mulatto! The year I was discovered with her brother in the love nest that Aunt Paula so obligingly lent us, Alexandra, my sister-in-law, so to speak, married a businessman from Venezuela. Like her, he had very little black blood in his veins. The whole town (me included, I must admit) gathered on the square in front of the cathedral. Every society has the gods it deserves. Ours are the mulattos. Not the Mandingo marabout's, of course. Good God, no! Not mine!

"What do they have over us? A little money they've accumulated in the shadiest of trades."

I don't agree. They do have something over us, however. They are free. Anyway, that's how I saw them. That was what I wanted to explain that evening, that famous evening. They were all sitting around, hissing.

"Marilisse! You're making yourself Marilisse!"

Due to his forthcoming departure, Sieur Cazeau, inhabitant of Cul de Sac, has put up for sale a young negro girl of pleasant features named Marilisse. Good laundress. Can be taken on a trial basis.

Nine years since I've been back.

I imagine my mother's face wrinkled. She never liked me very much. Anyway, she is my mother. She gave birth to me the afternoon of mardi gras. What a day to give birth! Outside the front door the masks danced and snapped their whips.

Bi à bi caiman
Mi guiab' là dého
Caïman
Bi à bi caïman
Mi guiab' là dého.

I uttered my first cry of terror and revolt. They were not very happy. They had wanted a boy. My mother, in a lace-embroidered nightdress, sighed. Friends leaned over:

"She's more . . . "

"She's less . . . "

"She doesn't look like the others."

The others, thank God! Now let's be serious.

Birame III laid down his *Principles* and accompanied me through the streets which were suddenly wildly alive. I recognize the sound of the balaphon, although it's not that familiar to me.

"He's a scholar, a wise man, a saint . . . "

Who? Saliou. Birame III has the intense admiration of adolescence. I like him, his youth, his emaciated face and high cheek bones.

Shall I offer him a boubou, a pair of shoes? No, he has asked nothing of me. He is proud and destitute. I must get rid of that dirty Christian habit of handing out money. After all, I haven't come here to give, but to receive. My hand is outstretched.

Yes, there's always Miss Lonelyhearts' explanations . . . Not yet. Let's get back to the first affair. Get it over with once and for all. Before going on to the second. In actual fact there's nothing much to say. I had a cycle, he a motorbike. We would meet at Aunt Paula's. How had I discovered Aunt Paula since the family no longer mentioned her? Premeditation, I must confess. When we had to find a roof, I thought of her. That's all . . . It's as simple as that and did not deserve all the secrecy they gave it. I was not doing a Marilisse. I was in love. That's all. A woman in love, isn't she always a Marilisse? Let the Feminists stone me if they want to!

What a beautiful scandal the affair caused! The Mandingo marabout had the best role in his career: the offended father! I left by plane, my legs all wobbly. Jean-Marie got married shortly afterwards. His family had had a near escape. I passed my baccalaureat with distinction in Paris, but the one did not rule out the other. They felt I ought not to go back. Spend the holidays in Switzerland or England, anywhere.

You see, Birame III, that's what's eating me. Not hunger or poverty or injustice in the world. He says goodbye at the hotel door. The hotel owner is there. A real brawler.

The next morning he's still there. With a cup of coffee instead of a glass of whisky. At his side, Marilisse, real name Adama. She chews on her toothpick and emits a strong odor (Blacks stink, everyone knows that).

"You know what Adama and me were saying last night. We were wondering what the hell a nice young thing like you was doing here."

Will they ever leave me in peace? I had a bad night. Not the tom-toms, that's for sure. Nor the din of the balaphon. Adama pours me a coffee. She has long painted nails edged with dirt. She's my sister, whether I like it or not. Both of us have shared the white man's bed. I've got a bad conscience. What about her? Oh no! For her it's obviously a big step up. No more millet to pound, eight months pregnant. And her baby will have blue eyes. With a bit of luck. Or a lot. I can swear this was not my case. I was in love. I mean the second time. The second man. The one who picked me up like a tart at Saint Germain. Unbelievable! He stuck his head through the car window.

"Wouldn't you like to have a drink?"

In all my life I have never let myself be accosted in the street. I was no longer at my wit's end, suicidal . . . But a quarter of an hour later, we were sitting face to face in one of those pseudo-English pubs.

"You're going to be bored to death in this hole!"

Adama pouted in approval. I bet she only dreams of Paris. Where the Sarakollé streetcleaners ply the pavements. She's not a Sarakollé, of course. I don't know if mine was either. He would look at us without hatred or disapproval.

Not like those West Indians at the Caribbean Festival.

What got me to go to such a place? Everything I usually run from:

biguine and punch. Probably nostalgia. Whatever you say, nine years is a long time. He was accompanying me, a little touch of exoticism . . . And there were these young West Indians with their Black Panther berets. All contempt. As in years before, all eyes on me.

And, as in years past, I opened my mouth to explain. Explain. They didn't hear a word. Their voices hissed:

"Marilisse! Marilisse!"

Aida and Jalla in Paris with their respective husbands, their children and their children's maids hadn't thought otherwise.

"Has he introduced you to his family?"

"To his mother?"

"To his father?"

"To his sisters?"

"How can you bear it?"

I tried to speak, to explain. They crushed me with contempt. And that's why I chose this country, supposed to be untouched by the West, far from the din of the Caravelles.

To stand back and get a look at myself.

The driver is asleep in his taxi. The hotel owner barks at him to wake him up. Why do they sleep so much? They sleep on the pavements. They sleep in the markets. They sleep on the doorsteps. Why? From hunger. They sleep from hunger.

This National Institute to which I had the bright idea of hiring my services does not look very sharp. A few mangy lawns. Two superb flame trees, however, and lots of mango trees in the yard. Some students in boubous are watching me. No use being afraid. They know nothing about me. Besides, their looks are full of kindness. One of them is smiling. So we have nine months together, a pregnancy, to discuss Marx, Kwame Nkrumah and other African avatars of Marxist doctrine. I'll do my best, even if I don't guarantee the result.

Saliou is in the yard.

"My wife's given birth. Another boy . . . "

His voice is full of pride. You do need girls though in this humble world to create boys. I'm sure if I had a child, boy or girl, it would be the same. But I've never had a child. In any case, I'll never have a child. Only little bastards.

"Don't be frightened. Everything will be alright, you'll see."

Does he take me for a child? I was a brilliant pupil at the lycée, populated by daddy's darlings, supposed to be difficult to handle. Because of me I'm sure there was a slight increase in tourists to the West Indies. It's not this ragged group of young students which is going to frighten me. And, as I said, they look as though they're ready to like me.

"Mademoiselle, which country are your from?"

Once again my first lecture here is going to be on the West Indies. The slave ships set off again from the Bight of Biafra. All that blood on the glazed eye of the sea. And those jolly sharks, jolly ancestors of the Ku Klux Klan.

"Hunt the nigger!"

They bombard me with questions. Birame III, who already looks like teacher's favorite, is sitting in the front row. The warmth in his eyes is doing me good. Why such a welcome? Is it simply the color of my skin? They're not interested in my family history. My past. It's nice though. One of them grows bold.

"Do you have a young sister? You must show us her picture."

They laugh. Me too. What are you frightened of Saliou? I have them eating out of my hand. They're trusting and naive. Basically, that was our downfall: trust and naiveté. The whites arrived with their glass beads and we gave them gold. Or men. Well, that's one version. I don't really believe it. There were crooks like Tegbessu who profited from the situation. He realized where we were going.

Birame III is waiting for me at the door. His friends look at him enviously.

"We have to go and see Oumou Hawa at the hospital. That's how we do it here."

We too. Circling round the cradle.

"She's more . . . "

"She's less . . . "

"She doesn't look like the others . . . "

My mother had a lace nightgown. I was crying at her breast. If I had been a boy then things would have been different. Is it as simple as that?

Birame III doesn't stop chattering. He has a slight stutter which has a certain charm. He's telling me there are two hospitals. The old

European hospital for the high officials of the young republic. The old native hospital, although renamed Jomo Kenyatta to illustrate African unity, serves the same purpose: care for those whose only riches can be measured in suffering. Nothing has changed, he tells me. Nothing.

"Salam malaikum."

"Malaikum Salam."

"Are you in peace?"

"Peace only."

"Are you in hunger?"

"Yes sister . . . Well, we don't really know, as we don't know anything else. Our fathers have squatted in front of this dish of rice and we can now help ourselves with our hands, after having washed them."

Women hold up their twins, their triplets, their quintuplets. God in his kindness only gives to the rich. A man with no legs wails in front of the maternity ward. Visitors go by without hearing.

Lots of people in Oumou Hawa's room. Men and women. Princesses from Belbourg in costly boubous. One of them is holding a baby in her arms. She looks like Oumou Hawa, decked out like a tournament horse, proud and sulky.

"Veronica, how kind. My sister Ramatoulaye . . . "

"Are you in peace?"

"Peace only."

"And in hunger?"

Oh no. Not these, they are princesses, it's obvious. We stare at each other fairly hard. Among women. They are beautiful, there's no doubt. Their eyes! Look out for clichés! Oumou Hawa explains. A chorus of voices.

"A teacher of philosophy? How nice!"

Ramatoulaye smiles. There is something reassuring in her smile.

"We won't ever let you go. We'll keep you here with us."

"We'll marrry you to a Fulani like us."

It might be a solution. The solution. The real return. Shaku Umar finds his mother again at Ber Kufa.

My son! My son!

She recognized him by his love.

For the time being the princesses have forgotten about me.

They're talking among themselves in their own language. Hermetic. A man enters. He isn't very tall. All the folds in his over-embroidered boubou don't manage to fill him out. Captain Snellgrave would not give much for this piece of Indies. Yet he has an extraordinary air of arrogance. Am I in the presence of an Oroonoko? It would be the first time, I do declare. They exchange their greetings slowly and langorously. So beautiful. The impression you get in church when the incense-soaked priests chant their endless salutations. The Oroonoko doesn't look at me, even when my presence is explained to him. What the hell am I doing here? What was I doing elsewhere? At least I made love. Every night. Jean-Michel was a bit anxious at first. He had heard so much about our sexual appetites. He was reassured. I was satisfied. Deuce.

Some believe sleeping with a black woman helps promote the cause of the underdog. They start talking with authority. He was never so naive, nor hypocritical. He would never place our coitus in the name of the Revolution. Besides, I'm not an underdog. Born with a silver spoon . . .

The princesses retire. The three of us remain, Oumou Hawa, the Oroonoko and myself. All four of us rather. I was forgetting the newly-born sleeping with his fists tightly clenched. Birame III is standing on the balcony. He is looking at the Oroonoko with hatred. Why?

He gives me a long explanation, his thin, dirty hand clasping my wrist. The Oroonoko is Oumou Hawa's brother.

"Her very own brother. Same mother, same father."

They descend from an old aristocratic family who with another royal family alternated their rule of a kingdom in the north in the pre-colonial period. Their history is so complicated. But I wasn't mistaken. He is an Oroonoko. Then their family became the staunchest ally of the colonial powers. Birame III gives a stark picture of the levies demanded by their grandfather and father. Taxes, forced labor for building roads or cash crops, nothing is missing from the picture. Whip in hand, they forced the laboring masses to work for the profit of the whites. And theirs too. Birame III cut his long story short. Tell me about this Oroonoko. His real name is Ibrahima Sory. El Hadj since he's been to Mecca.

Birame III gets even more worked up.

"He's the Minister for the Defense and the Interior. An assassin. His hands are dripping with the blood of the people."

These children do have a vocabulary! It's obvious they don't read the right books. At his age I was reading *Les Liaisons Dangeureuses.* It is healthier even so. Let's be serious. Quite frankly, I don't care a damn for the past and present crimes of this aristocratic family. They are the ones I came to see. Genuine aristocrats. Not monkeys. Grandsons of slaves dancing the minuet and despising those who did not have as much luck or skill in the race for 'humanity.' This nigger has ancestors!

Birame III is now dragging me off to the Ho Chi Minh estate where his guardian lives. What a pompous name. In actual fact it's a muddle of small houses in concrete squared off around communal concessions. Rubbish piles up at every crossroad. Women are selling fried plantain in palm oil. Birame III's guardian, naked to the waist and wearing baggy trousers, is surrounded by friends and drinking beer in a stuffy little room. He rushes into his bedroom to find a shirt. His wife rushes out of the kitchen, a baby on her back and another in her skirts. Three others file behind. Let us reproduce!

"Mademoiselle is Birame III's teacher?"

"Could Mademoiselle say which country she comes from?"

"Could Mademoiselle say where this country is?"

"What a strange country which has no Mandingo, no Fulani, no Toucouleur, no Serer, no Woloff, no Toma, no Guerze, no Fang, no Fon, no Bété, no Fanti, no Baoulé, no Ewe, no Dagbani, no Yoruba, no Mina, no Ibo. And yet the inhabitants are black."

"Are all the women of this country as pretty as Mademoiselle?"

I got a silly pleasure out of hearing this. What do you expect, I still have a complex from my awkward days of childhood. Years of being downgraded in comparison with my two sisters. That's probably why I took refuge in protest. Had the Mandingo marabout bounced me more often on his knee and called *me* his little pearl, like Aida and Jalla, I would most likely not be here today. He is the one with whom I have an account to settle. My mother never impressed me very much. She was just a moon round the paternal planet.

"Could Mademoiselle tell us about Paris?"

Paris! No, not me.

Ask your brothers. One of them sweeps the street by the rue de l'Université and looks at us every morning. Me and my white man. No contempt in his look, and that's what I can't get out of my mind.

Paris? What can I say about Paris? Anyway my Paris wouldn't be yours. Yours is the tall, dark plastic dustbins and the short, phosphorescent jackets in the dawn. Yours is the weekends, playing pinball in the cafés, whose owners are fed up. All these niggers and the other colored customers have fled.

I get up. I don't belong here. They ask me to stay. A small boy has run to the corner of the street. I have to drink the lukewarm beer in a mustard glass.

The hotel proprieter isn't that bad after all. He absolutely insists that I tell him all about my broken heart. That's what brought me here, he is convinced. If I had a broken heart, I'd choose a country that has a *joie de vivre*. Not this place that stinks of poverty. Poverty yet dignity, I must admit. Even the beggars have a dignified look. The blind with their eyes turned skywards led by dirty little boys. Adama isn't a bad girl either. She has a strong smell, that's all and that isn't a crime. Perhaps Jean likes that. He's called Jean, the hotel proprietor. Jean Lefevre. He's from Rouen. He has never read Flaubert. Him, read! The main thing is that he knows how to count. Adama has already told him he's mean and she has to beg him to pay for her dresses. If Jean-Michel could see me!

"Don't tell me you left me for an aperitif with a bartender and a whore!"

Why whore? Because she goes to bed with a white man?

Jean Lefevre offers a second pastis. I refuse. I'd better go up to my room for a good siesta, the heat is unbearable. The hotel stewards have got the knack. They sleep rolled up in a ball like a foetus in the tiled corridors. The one I am stepping over has a look of terror on his face. What is he dreaming about under his closely-shaven skull?

Naturally if Jean-Michel saw me he would laugh. He would ask me to stop acting the fool. My cases are still unpacked. Take the next DC-10 back in the opposite direction. He will be waiting for me amidst the screams of the Boeings.

Somebody is knocking at my door. Perhaps I slept. In any case, I didn't dream. Africa has already given me one thing—a dreamless sleep. A young, immaculately dressed soldier is standing to attention on the threshold. Am I dreaming? Let's see what crimes have I committed? Nothing that can get me arrested manu militari it seems.

"I'm the Minister's chauffeur."

Is this a clue?

"The Minister would like to speak with you."

What minister? And on what subject, my good friend? He smiles.

I was warned in Paris. There are always some people better informed than others. Whose aunt, uncle or nephew has spent two weeks in Chad or Sudan—those African countries, they're police states where anything can happen—imprisonment for no reason, torture, reprisals under the guise of legislation. Perhaps my presence here has drawn suspicion. And it is suspicious, let's face it. I follow my soldier who courteously stands back to let me pass on the stairs and opens the door of the Mercedes.

Nobody sees me leave. Adama and Jean Lefevre are taking their siesta. As for the stewards, it's no use counting on them. Am I frightened? No, since I have a clear conscience. To tell the truth, I don't have a clear conscience. Let's be logical. This type of crime, if any, is not the affair of a civil or military court. I lean over and ask. I have the right to know where they are taking me. Answer.

"To Heremakhonon."

Is this a clue? The surroundings change. The Jet Tour brochures are true after all. It's the African Riviera. The baobabs are hundreds of years old. The flame trees are magnificent. And they're mine. They border the roads of my island from the north to the south and bleed onto the roofs of our huts. Nine years!

We pass by a high gate carved with a sun. A flag is flying. The guards are armed to the teeth.

"Mwalimwana's villa."

There's a song about Mwalimwana. I heard it on the radio. In fact you hear it four times a day with a balaphon background and kora accompaniment.

Mwalimwana notre père
Mwalimwana est venu
Mwalimwana ce que tu fais me plaît
Mwalimwana je te salue
Mwalimwana, roi des hommes forts.

He's entitled to guards at his door. And to a song. He threw the whites into the sea, didn't he? Something that Tegbessu and his likes were unable to do. Now that the whites are in the sea, though, his people continue to die of hunger. They are free, though. Apparently this is very important.

The Mercedes turns into a drive perpendicular to the sea. A long low white villa—Heremakhonon. A servant comes out.

"Salam malaikum."

"Malaikum Salam."

He shows me into the house. Suddenly, as I sit down, something gives inside me. The tension with which I have obviously been living over the past weeks, months, years, breaks. Perhaps it is the utter coolness of this room or its silence? In this town you forget what silence is, the sound of the drums, the pounding of the pestles, the melodious voice of the balaphon and from time to time the high, raw voice of the muezzin. Here, all is silence. Heremakhonon is an island, off the course of the Santa Maria—no syphilis for the future Red Skins. I close my eyes, perhaps sleep. Ibrahima Sory enters. Without his ceremonial dress he is even thinner and frailer. He smiles and apologizes for having summoned me in such an offhand manner. It doesn't matter. We converse. What does he want?

"I hear you do not yet have accommodations?"

That doesn't matter either. I am not like my expatriate friends in the staff room who are dying for a house with a garden, and not too far from the sea. I am not looking for amenities in Africa. Besides, Adama and Jean Lefevre are perfect companions.

"Do you intend to buy a car?"

Here I have to laugh. A car? Rather a bicycle or a solex at the very most, to cause the least damage. To get around without running over sheep, women and children crossing the street at the most unexpected moments. Without crashing into the blind and crippled intoning the Koran wherever the whim takes them. No, Mr. Minister, sir, you can keep your car. In emergencies there's Saliou's Skoda. It always starts when you push it. I am not a standard expatriate. That's obvious, isn't it? This man is handsome. That doesn't mean anything. Eva Braun no doubt thought Hitler handsome. I think him handsome. His eyes are proud and sad. And I like his air of arrogance. What does he want? Nothing it seems. Extreme courtesy. I am a foreigner encountered at his sister's bedside. He asks if I am being well looked after.

"Do you like our country?"

Like? I really don't know. I'm an invalid, Mr. Minister, seeking therapy. I could tell you a lot. But he's getting up. Apparently the conversation is over.

"I'll do my best to make you feel at home."

In a way he keeps his word. Who says these African ministers have a one-track mind?

Less than twelve hours after this visit, Jean Lefevre, Adama and myself are having lunch together (you don't expect me to eat alone, Jean-Michel) when two soldiers arrive with a mass of papers to sign. I have been allocated a villa. Adama screams with joy. Jean Lefevre makes a face.

"You're holding something from us, ma petite."

Where is this villa?

Strange how this town is stratified! I caught a quick glimpse of the ministerial paradise. There are also embassies and foreign missions. I have been given asylum in this kind of no-man's land of French and American technical assistants up in arms against each other and among each other—Poles, Czechs, Russians and Chinese. Don't forget Mwalimwana is non-aligned! Provided they leave me alone. I haven't crossed the oceans to get mixed up in their quarrels. There is a small garden in front of the villa and the earth is rich and red. I could plant flowers.

My mother used to put on her gloves, a large straw hat and arm herself with pruning shears.

Aida and Jalla used to trot round her. She would shout:

"Mind my pansies!"

We used to send armfuls of flowers to the village for the altar on Corpus Christi. That was at Hérone where we had our country house and fifteen acres of land. Our caretaker was a sad coolie called Verassamy. A gawky old nomad, unaccustomed to the town, looms up.

"My name's Abdourahmane."

Is this a clue? He says he cooks, launders, and irons. It's yours, Abdourahame.

Strangely enough when I see Saliou and Birame III again I feel like lying to make them believe I don't know where this villa comes from. Saliou is slightly surprised. Birame III a lot. Priority housing is given to large families, those who transport their kids, their baby food, their bottles by DC-10. I lie therefore. Something I do rarely. Why?

I do it badly. It would be easy to trip me up. But Saliou and Birame III are preoccupied. They explain that Mwalimwana will make the rounds of the schools. The show must be in style.

Mwalimwana notre père,
Mwalimwana tu es beau,
Ce que tu fais me plaît.

The tune is lovely. Why does it irritate them both? Naturally, they are full of explanations. Unfortunately I am not very attentive. I didn't come to get mixed up in a debate on African socialism. I must rid myself of these *rab* and send them back to Sangomar. Which is my *ndöp*?

Perhaps it's all much ado about nothing. Sometimes I tell myself this and try to be logical. Once again, I loved these two men because I was in love. All those young black males that my family introduced me to made me shudder. Why? Not because they were black. Ridiculous! I'm no Mayotte Capécia. No! I'm not interested in whitening the race! I swear . . . But it's what they thought. What the others thought of me. Obviously I could have laughed at their Black Panther berets and their black leather jackets. Paris isn't New York. Laugh? I didn't think of it.

I open my mouth to explain. Explain what? I wake up soaked. For a first night in my little villa, it's not a great success. The African night is as opaque as the womb.

Why did I lie to Saliou and Birame III? I guessed they wouldn't appreciate this favor from the people's assassin. As they call him. I'm sick of labels. The truth is I am attracted to him, this nigger with ancestors. And it's the first time. Emmanuel, son of the first or second black doctor, Charles André, son of the second chemist, black of course, Déodat, son of the third dentist, black again! They came in their shiny shoes for the doll's christening. Something blocked inside me. And I put on such a severe unfriendly face that they retreated. Strange this conversation I had with Dr. Hypollite. Dr. Hypollite is my eldest sister's husband. They say he is handsome because his features are hardly negroid. Except for the mouth. We were waiting then for Aida to try on a cocktail dress at a fashion designer for oversized women, rue du Colisée, as she had put on quite a bit of weight since her marriage. Between us sat their eldest son, Marc-Antoine, three years old and my godson. We do have a sense of the family. Aida never liked me very much. I am her sister, however. I have to be godmother to her eldest son.

"If you had wanted to," Dr. Hypollite said.

Wanted what? I looked at him and understood. If he had wanted to I could have been in his bed under his repeated assaults; Aida whispers he lays it on hard. I would be the one buying cocktail dresses for oversized women, having put on too much weight. I would be Marc-Antoine's mother, quite adorable by the way. God forbid!

"Instead of that . . . "

He suffocates. Yes, I know, I know. Instead of that, I turned myself into a Marilisse with a mulatto who, caught virtually in mid-coitus, has not made up my honor. And now, if that was not enough .

"This Jean-Michel, if he loves you, he should marry you and face up to the world."

Big words, always big words.

This sort of person is basically naive. That's why they are happy. They are, aren't they?

"Happy?"

Dr. Hypollite gets perturbed. Two years ago he launched into politics. He will end up a deputy in the National Assembly.

"You know what we say. Happiness is the blossom of the cotton tree. Now you see it, now you don't."

Marc-Antoine spills his ice-cream over his knee which creates a welcome diversion.

So it's the first time. Yes, the first. I'm not sleepy anymore. Besides, it's too hot. Will the sun ever rise?

Of course. It's been rising for generations. Without seeming to tire. It will rise, especially as it's the day of Mwalimwana's visit.

Even Birame III has smartened himself up and put on the boubou that I offered him in the end (please forgive me) and has shaved his head. There is nobody at his guardian's to do the washing. He washes his boubou himself and waits for it to dry with a simple cloth around his waist. He does his homework by candlelight, as they have cut the electricity—the guardian hasn't paid for three months.

At 9:30 a.m. sirens wail (Mwalimwana is punctual) and all the students flock to the windows. Then they start counting.

"One Lincoln Continental. One, two, three, four, five, six Mercedes."

They make me laugh. Do they expect Mwalimwana to ride around on a bicycle like the King and Queen of Denmark? The King and Queen of Denmark have got nothing more to prove, Mwalimwana has. A shepherd *cum* father of the nation has to give a show of ostentation. Have these children heard of Christophe, the former slave? And his court? He had to prove over and over again that he was civilized.

"Mademoiselle, Mademoiselle, Mwalimwana is sure to come into our classroom. He loves talking about Marx."

He comes in at ten minutes past ten. Part of his escort remains in the corridor chatting. Saliou accompanies him, tense. Good-looking. Yes. Good-looking, Mwalimwana, slightly overweight perhaps. He's starting to put on weight, like the rich. A threat of coronorary thrombosis. He smiles at me.

"From the West Indies? Well, that's nice. One of the children that Africa lost . . . "

Sold, Mwalimwana, sold. Not lost. Tegbessu got 400 pounds sterling per boat load.

" . . . and found again. Are you pleased with our students' work?"

They don't do a damn thing. All they think of doing is criticizing your behavior.

"Hard-working, you say? But sometimes a little slapdash? Shake them up. We spoil them too much. Free primary and secondary schooling. Free university education too. Free dispensaries for medical care. You know what it was like under the white man: bush schools where you grilled under the corrugated iron roof. Koranic schools where you learned by heart, occasionally casting an eye at the written page . . . "

And yet, Mwalimwana, they're not content. I've already realized that. They count your Mercedes and vent their anger against your wives' jewels. They say an oligarchy of greed has taken over from Europe. Instead of the Koran they recite Fanon. Yesterday they wanted to drag me into a discussion of *The Wretched of the Earth* that I haven't read. Mea culpa! Mea maxima culpa!

"We must make unceasing efforts to find our own paths of development if we want to achieve our revolution without altering our personality . . . "

Everybody makes speeches. Mwalimwana's isn't any worse than the others. I would say it's better than most of those I used to hear at our Sub-Prefect's. The students have a glazed look about them.

The door closes. In all it hadn't lasted more than ten minutes. Much ado . . . no, it seems it isn't over.

There's going to be a play in amphitheater C and then . . . I didn't come this far to be bored to death by a school play, shake hands and have my picture taken. I've had my fill of this sort of function. You only have to look at the Mandingo marabout's photo album. Prefects, ministers for overseas territories, bishops and, the top prize, a dedicated photo of Eboué in full morning dress dating from his short stay as governor of the island. I am going home.

Oh, the sun! What an unfeeling god who never shuts an eyelid. Who forces its supplicants to endure its stare. Allah, pity! I've already realized that giving alms means giving away one's salary. I have even learned to thrust aside with a strong hand beggars who are too enterprising. It's Birame III who taught me, learnedly explaining that individual charity is useless and that it is no answer to poverty. My coins are a drop in the ocean. Their only purpose is to give me a clear conscience. We need a revolution, dixit Birame III. After his idol comes Saliou. What a pair the two of them make!

Perhaps he'll be offended if I dodge the play and the reception in honor of Mwalimwana? I've always offended anyway. And that's why I am here. Now don't let's start all over again.

I've begun to like this town, like a man whose ugliness, clumsiness and shyness grows on you. In their destitution these people have kept a certain beauty. How? I don't know. I am under its spell, like all beauty.

Friday, the day of the mosque. Broadcasting house is opposite a mosque. Revolutionary songs and verses from the Koran alternate. Contrasts, contrasts. I disappear into the house. Abdourahamane has the annoying habit of inviting his whole family to my kitchen during mealtimes. But his children are so adorable that I haven't the heart to protest.

"Salam malaikum."

"Malaikum salam."

One of them is called Fodé. He has tiny teeth blackened by too much fluoride in the water back home. He doesn't speak a word of French. I have bought him some colored crayons. Can't get over the habit of giving. He is drawing on the walls. I'm going to take a siesta like everybody else in this hole. It's because of the sun. What else can you do? Go to the beach with my fellow expatriates and bake under the sun? My assimilation doesn't go that far. Just when I'm about to retire a young soldier arrives.

"The Minister . . . "

I must confess my heart skips a beat. I'm beginning to think it's not just the concern for a foreigner's well-being. At least I hope so.

The Mercedes that Abdourahamane's children are stroking shoots off.

When we get to Den Bata mosque we pass Saliou's Skoda. My instinct tells me to hide myself. Why, for goodness sake?

Oh, disappointment. Ibrahima Sory is not at home. Abdoulaye, the houseboy, eyes to the ground, explains that he has been called to the President's palace, but should not be long and asks me to wait. Can you imagine a lovers' tryst where one of the partners is absent? Is it a lovers' tryst? Abdoulaye brings me a grapefruit juice and magazines the way they do at the dentist's. What if I were to go home? Stop kidding yourself . . . It is obvious that nothing will make me budge. That I'll wait. This house has charm. Charm in the literal sense of the word. You breathe it in or drink it in the grapefruit juice. I don't really know where it's hiding, but it's there. This armchair gives me an extraordinary feeling of well-being. Time stands still. The clock is going back. I'm five. I'm in the kitchen. I'm watching Mabo Julie make the evening meal. She is singing.

Surah en blanc,
Ka semb'on pigeon blanc
Surah en gris
Ka semb'on tourterelle.

She has a great big face that I saw fifteen years later on Scarlett

O'Hara's maid. There's another servant in the kitchen. A thin, yellow-skinned girl . . . A quadroon. I'm ten. I'm lying on the pebbles by the River Rose. People are splashing happily in the water. Mabo Julie calls me:

"Come on, Chouboulou à maman."

Sweet, sickly-sweet images. I haven't been back for nine years. I imagine my mother is white-haired. The Mandingo marabout is still as straight as a die. They are waiting for me at the airport.

"What have you been doing all this time?"

I wanted to run away—run away—run away.

Ibrahima Sory appears. He apologizes for having made me wait so long. So long? I thank him for having allocated me a villa. He waves this aside. We talk. What does he want? The most thick-headed woman is capable of guessing whether a man wants her. This case is unfathomable. He is courteous, indifferent, even slightly bored. There are long silences, which only seem to embarrass *me.* This man could be a marabout's spell. It's obvious he's not very concerned about it. He gets up.

"I have to go back to the palace. Could you wait for me? Make yourself at home."

Abdoulaye reappears and this time offers me mint tea. How long am I going to stay here and wait? This is ridiculous . . . Abdoulaye puts a record on. On the floor is an animal skin. And leather poofs, hand-made. In Kano, the Hausa city, they dye cloths in indigo. Girls with slanting eyes offer red rice to passers-by.

Two young boys enter. The older, very arrogant, almost hostile. The younger, chubby and debonnaire. They look at me. Are they related to the Minister? The older is his own brother, the younger, the son of his half-brother. In short, it's the same all over. The difference is that Heremakhonon and its outhouses can house two villages. And there's no risk of the electricity being cut off like at Birame III's guardian's. If Birame III and Saliou could see me.

What am I waiting for here and why? I've lost track. Night has fallen. It's pitch black. I used to be afraid of the dark. The *Bête à Man Hibé* is coming, cloppity, cloppity, clop. Mabo Julie laughs at my fright. She takes me to the end of the terrace.

"Look, look!"

Oh, the branches of the ylang, ylang tree are full of shapes. Let's go out into the garden . . . Footsteps behind me.

"Did I frighten you?"

I'm past the age. You intrigue me, it's not the same. I crossed the seas for you, you know. Just for you. It would be easy to speak in the shadows. Abdoulaye serves more mint tea and leaves. Do you understand? But am I making myself clear? Let's start again. I detested them because they weren't free. Because they were terribly afraid of being what it was said they were. Because, in fact, they thought they were just that. And I felt it. I have always felt it. How? Don't ask me how. I felt it, that's all. Can you understand? That was it. The people I loved never had that fear. They were free. To be themselves. Genuinely; deep down. Jean-Marie, dunce from the first form to the sixth. Not an iota of intelligence. Jean-Michel, lazy and unconventional. They had nothing to prove. They were my freedom. I mean it was through them that I got there. Obviously the family got it all wrong. And now I'm having doubts. Supposing they were right? Yes. If it was nothing else but a lot of excuses?

"You will stay, won't you?"

I haven't waited two hours for nothing. It would be a sad affair to have to retrace my steps in your Mercedes deluxe. He pours some more tea. The liquid is poured from one receptacle to another several times and there's this little sound of running water. I feel good and I'd like to talk. Listen.

Our house was one of the prettiest in town. It had a balcony, high windows and bougainvillea on the balcony. My nurse was called Mabo Julie, she used to wear starched petticoats under her dress. She loved me. She would always stand up for me and gave me great slices of angel cake in the kitchen. And cups of chodo. Unfortunately, she died when I was sixteen. That same year I was initiated to love and death.

"Abdoulaye will show you your room. I'll join you in a moment."

My attempt at a true confession is struck dead. I have already been in a number of incongruous situations. But this one beats them all. I am going to bed with a perfect stranger. Well, we always make love to a stranger as incest is forbidden. But the barriers are broken with flowers and words. Courting in others words. Even short-lived.

Or Jean-Michel's anti-flirt in a pub for anglophiles.

"I'm not used to picking up women in the street. You do believe me, don't you? But I am very attracted to you."

In situations like that I'm at ease. In the present case, I'm out of my depths. May as well get undressed and slip into this deep bed with dark blue sheets. It will be less embarrassing than undressing in front of each other. When he comes. If only he would hurry up . . . Time here hasn't the same meaning.

"Were you asleep?"

Almost. He smiles.

"Strange, you look like a girl from my village."

Whom you loved?

I'm sorry. I studied Marivaux at school.

He laughs, half in kindness, half in derision.

"You're not in Europe here."

Which means what? He bites on a small brown nut.

"Have you ever tasted a kola nut?"

I confess I haven't. Is this in answer to my question? He laughs again, leans over and kisses me.

This man who is about to take me does not know that I am a virgin of sorts. Of course the wrapper won't be stained with blood and the griotte won't hold it up proudly to reassure the tribe. It will be another blood. Heavier and thicker. Before letting it flow, black and fast, I now realize why he fascinates me. He hasn't been branded.

Pierre Kotokoli, branded on the right breast 'LA' with illegible writing underneath. 'Au Cap' on the left breast. 'FIESS' below 'St M.'

He'll get the *rab* to leave my body and return to the Sangomar point. No need to oil my body and bury myself in cloth. Tell me you understand me, my nigger with ancestors. Their whole life was a secret struggle, a struggle for life against something they thought hidden in their very soul. Lurking like a fetid beast. That had to be destroyed. And yet they rambled on. Oh, how they rambled. I can hear them now.

"We have proved that our Race . . . "

Our Race, our Race, our Race. You can understand why Race was coming out of my ears.

That's why.

Am I talking? Or do I think I'm talking? I must be dreaming as he doesn't answer.

He switches on the lamp, which is not made of shea butter, and looks at his watch. At this time of night?

"I have to go now."

Go where? Doesn't he know that sleeping together brings you closer? He dresses quickly and meticulously.

"There's work to be done. And I have to get up early for prayer."

A believer, if I understand correctly. Tough luck for me. At the door he asks considerately:

"You're not afraid?"

Who does he think I am? I've been used to the dark for ages. Man Hibé's horse has been silenced.

Marabout, marabout, you too. Seated on his sheepskin, he pleads his defense and shakes his head.

"I told you it would be long."

He laughs showing his toothless gums.

"You're too much in a hurry. Too much in a hurry, like the white man."

What do you expect, like Master . . . Frustrated is the word.

Not physically, of course. You could say I'm blessed in this respect. Dissatisfied. Unhappy even. Worse, I feel like crying like a child who doesn't know what's the matter. What did I expect? . . . Next time . . . Will there be a next time? I don't even know whether I want there to be one.

The driver stops. We have arrived at the Institute although I have no desire to work. What did I expect? It's obvious: to talk. Why do I want to talk to him and nobody else? I've already said why.

I'm like those old church hens who set their heart on a confessor. My mother would only confess with Father Michaud because she liked his eyes. Can you imagine? Saliou's managerial office is deserted. Silence. What's going on?

There are, as I have already said, some lovely mango trees in the Institute's courtyard. The students have taken refuge in their branches and are screaming, yelping, whistling and hissing. Those who didn't find room in the leaves have formed crazy circles around the trunks. What on earth is going on?

"They're on strike!"

Strike! Why?

"Their comrades have been arrested."

Arrested?

"Didn't you know?"

My expatriate colleagues fill me in. To crown yesterday's visit by Mwalimwana, the students put on a play of their own making. It dealt with a country whose people were groaning under dictatorship. The Minister for Agricultural Development was nicknamed the Starver of the Peasants, the Minister of the Defense and Interior, the Great Assassin, the Minister for Foreign Affairs, the Beggar for Foreign Aid and the Mwalimwana himself, the Great Exploiter. All innocent fun! A schoolboy prank. The pupils at the Lycée Condorcet depict their president with a vacuum cleaner and Paris students liken the U.S. President to a wild beast.

"The context is not the same. We are in a young republic here."

Young? Scholars claim that Africa is the cradle of humanity. In any case, Mwalimwana and his Politburo did not think at all along the same lines. After the show, not one sign of disapproval. He shook hands and congratulated them on their talent. Then, at the end of the afternoon, the soldiers arrived. They summoned the students responsible for each section and carted them off in handcuffs.

No sense of humor, Mwalimwana!

If the heads of state had to put away everyone who ran them down! But perhaps this does passeth my understanding.

In any case, the sight of these children stuck up in trees is ridiculous. Make them get down. Have you ever heard of a strike in history where the students turn into mangoes, green or otherwise? If this goes on, I'm going home. Suddenly it hits me. Birame III is responsible for the Philosophy Section. Well?

Like the others. Arrested. My little Birame III, all bone and chatter, arrested! Like the others . . . It becomes less of a farce and I no longer feel like laughing. They mustn't hurt this child, one of my first allies, my first friend along with Saliou. A thin, slender man dressed in a Mao suit emerges. I'm told he is responsible for the Youth Section. What a lot of responsibilities in this country! He is accompanied by the vice-head and several other men. Where is Saliou in all this? He should be here. In the meantime, a shower of mangoes greets the man and his disciples. He doesn't let himself be perturbed. The message is clear. It's the same for all rebels. Lay down you arms, your guns, your stones or your mangoes *first.* Then we'll see.

Where is Saliou? At the palace, I am told, with a delegation of students trying to see Mwalimwana. Frankly, isn't this all much ado about nothing? If Mwalimwana had found the joke slightly sour, couldn't he have given out extra homework lines or something? No, straightaway, the high-handed behavior! Soldiers and all the tra-la-la. No sense of humor at all. And now it's getting out of hand.

At ten a.m. the army trucks start arriving. High, dark green trucks. Let's be honest. It's not very impressive. The soldiers have their guns slung over their shoulders. Their uniforms are made in Egypt. Their arms in the U.S.A. Trained by Russians. Lest we forget, Mwalimwana is non-aligned. Believe me, it's not bad being a soldier. The pay is good. You live in camp with your wife and your children, free electricity and water. Your wife no longer has to line up at the water fountain. You can send money back to the village and, when you're on leave, your uniform gives you prestige, status. Sometimes, you build roads with the Germans. Bridges with the Chinese. The Chinese are clever. Cleverer it seems than the white man. And us, when will we be cleverer than the Chinese and the white man?

When the trucks arrive there is a moment of panic. Students and mangoes fall out of the trees. The crazy circles around the trunks stop. The man from the youth section and his disciples are back and resume the chant:

"However just your claims may be . . . "

Come on, get down! Be reasonable and stop being mangoes!

"Last warning!"

The soldiers jump out of their trucks and point their guns. All chaos lets loose. It starts raining students. Then lifting up their boubous they run towards the amphitheaters, knocking into each other. The soldiers pick up those who fall in the scrum.

"Brothers, don't act the fool. You've got books, exercise books for writing. Study, that's all you're asked to do. All your talk about equality and justice. Was there equality and justice when the white man was here? They whipped you and that was that. Brothers, you don't realize your good fortune."

One of them is crying and hiding his face with a fold in his boubou. Who is he crying for? For his pals who were arrested and whom he couldn't help? What can children do against the barrel of a gun? Even as a bluff. All this of course is a bluff.

"Not at all."

Now Saliou, you can't expect me to believe they would have fired on defenseless children. They wanted to frighten them and they did. They'll soon let Birame III and the others go, with their heads down and their tails between their legs. A rather tough lesson. Saliou is nervous. He keeps coming and going.

"Provided nothing happens to these children!"

No, of course not. Sit down. Relax. Let's have a talk. He looks at me.

"Where were you yesterday evening? I stopped by twice."

Where? With Jean Lefevre and Adama.

This lie comes out quite naturally. Why? Why this feeling of guilt? And it is guilt.

He pouts.

"Can't you find any other friends apart from that filthy colonialist and his whore?"

I protest. Aren't I free to do what I like? I can't help trembling. If he knew the truth . . . He would never understand that the political person of Ibrahima Sory leaves me cold. And his role in the nation. And his family's. I didn't come to get mixed up in their quarrels and take sides. I came to find a cure. Ibrahima Sory, I know, will be the marabout's *gree-gree.* We'll exchange our childhoods and our past. Through him I shall at last be proud to be what I am. He wasn't branded. You can see that. I have already resumed hope. At least I'm trying.

"Your incomprehension of this country's situation is heartbreaking. As for your indifference . . ."

Saliou, give me the credit of not trying to lie. I know it is fashionable to affect a certain jargon, certain ideas. I am a poor actress. I don't feel at ease in a borrowed personality. I told you immediately who I was.

He sits down, despondent. He looks at me.

"I would like to make you understand. Do you know how many political prisoners there are?"

Oh, let's talk about something else. These are not my worries./ Mine? Please, let's not think about them.

Dusk is falling. The bats are starting to gather above the cotton trees. Birame III will spend his night on bread and water. It won't do him any harm. It will even teach him not to criticize his elders so much. Does he think they have it that easy?

"Are you coming home for dinner?"

Oumou Hawa has begun to fascinate me as well and I would like to ask her so many questions. Ask her how a daughter of the noble and powerful Almanys family was married in obscurity to a revolutionary who is not from the same ethnic group. I imagine a wild passion, fighting to survive. I'm not entirely wrong. Saliou told me one day that he has no dealings with his wife's family. But Oumou Hawa talks very little. She is always busy with one of her children.

I sit on a stool and watch her stir the sauce with a large wooden spoon. At Saliou's there are about a dozen mouths to feed each day. She smiles at me.

"Ramatoulaye would like to see you again."

There's no doubt about it, the whole family likes me. From the brothers to the sisters. Flattery, when it comes down to it. The sauce perfumes the air.

"She thinks you look like a girl from our village."

I've already been told that. Oumou Hawa, tell me about your village. She laughs. Describe it!

"There's nothing to describe. It's like all the others. I'm sure you'd be bored to death. There are no amusements, nothing."

Who's talking of amusements? She looks at me maliciously.

"Have you ever slept on a mat on the ground? It's very cold where we live; it's on the high plateau in the North."

Everything she says gets me even more excited. What wouldn't I give to be born in the North? My father sitting on his sheepskin receiving homage from his vassals. He never talks of Race. Can there be another one apart from ours? The whites are but uncircumcised dogs. She laughs again and says something to Saliou who comes closer and sits between us.

"I'll take you to the North."

Oh no, I won't go with you. You'd be the wrong sort of guide. You only think in terms of standard of living, malnutrition, infant mortality and land reform. You'd say: "Here they should have built a school. Or a hospital." You only think of material things.

He is about to explode, then shrugs his shoulders as if he has second thoughts.

"Don't let's quarrel."

This evening the house is full of comings and goings. A tangle of suppositions about Birame III and the other student leaders dominates. Shouldn't I feel more concerned? Some of them have been told from a reliable source that Mwalimwana is planning to organize a mass meeting tomorrow at the Party Headquarters. There he will demand public criticism of these children before they pledge allegiance to the Revolution. This doesn't seem particularly harsh. A little surprising. Each country has its methods.

"Birame III will never accept."

He would be stupid not to. Galileo denied and swore that it didn't turn on its axis. And then the future proved him right.

"He's a proud, stubborn child. He has suffered a lot."

Poor Birame III! It's true he has suffered. I would have liked to give him back his childhood. But which one? Not mine. I'm still working mine out of my system. All those images and thoughts filling up my head. He has to listen to me.

"Even the worst dictatorships of Latin America don't unleash their soldiers against students."

Oh, excuse me, they do. I read the papers like everyone else, and I read reports of mass arrests and tortures. But unleash, let's not exaggerate. It was all bluff. Blackmail by the barrel of a gun. That's all.

In other words, even if I'm not good at explaining, you haven't understood, have you? They say I am the shame of the family. They say they gave me everything, education, breeding. But that I'm wallowing in the mud out of a shameful group instinct. You can understand that it is not true. The mud is in them.

Even so, nine years is a long time.

They must have forgotten since. Or else they'll pretend to forget. Perhaps they'll whisper a bit behind my back. Not very serious. We'll pay visits. They'll open bottles of Pol Roger in my honor. I'll have a place at the university and my pew in the central aisle if I want.

I was ten. Adolpha. She had come back from Bordeaux where she had been studying medicine. God forgive me, she was so ugly! Her parents were a couple of honorary primary school teachers who had been deserving members of the Race.

Everyone was chattering. The tablecloth was white. The crystal was sparkling. Inside me a wave rose, swelled up, broke and with one blow I pushed the table with both feet. What a wonderful mess!

"Why on earth?"

Three days locked in my room. Mabo Julie, sore at heart, entered on tiptoe.

"You know why you did that?"

"I couldn't listen to them any more."

We give thanks to our Lord for having made us different from the other niggers. And equal to the white man, our former master. Amen! As Saliou's Skoda refuses categorically to start, one of his friends accompanies me. He is a lecturer of political science at the Institute. I noticed him once or twice between classes.

"I am afraid for these children. Mwalimwana is the most savage monster in history . . . "

What exaggerations! Let's have a sense of proportion! Hitler was much more dangerous. All this is very confusing in the long run. Exactly what do they reproach Mwalimwana for? Perhaps I should try and understand.

"His close collaborators are corrupt and bloodthirsty, prepared to do anything to hold onto their power. The worst of all is Ibrahima Sory . . . "

I give a start.

"The worst because he is the most intelligent. We were together at the university. Then they catapulted him as Minister in place of his feudal father who refused to leave his fief in the north . . . "

Just my luck. I have a knack for getting myself into awkward situations. Why out of all of them did I have to be attracted to this man? Obviously, I couldn't be attracted to another.

Abdourahamane, his family and in-laws are in great conversation in the garden. Palaver, they say. What about? No idea. It's symbolic. I have no idea what is going on in this country. What is more I don't want to know. Is that possible? For the time being, yes. For how long?

Birame III on bread and water . . . Ibrahima Sory assassin of the people. I don't want to know. I don't. I don't. Is it possible?

In one way or another you are attracted to events, magnetized by them as if they had their own force, a will of their own. I don't want to, but it's impossible.

I'm already trapped. Already? Otherwise would I be where I am?

The hall of the Party Headquarters, which has housed the glorious meetings of the fight for independence, is bursting at the seams. The students and secondary school pupils in the front rows. On the benches in the side aisles, the Party's women militants, turbaned matrons, who they say are the pillars of Mwalimwana's throne. Spasmodically they sing the famous:

Mwalimwana est venu
Mwalimwana ce que tu fais me plait
Mwalimwana je te salue
Mwalimwana roi des hommes forts.

Some of the pupils and students sing with them. Naturally I am not singing. Even so, I am here. Why? It's obvious. I'm concerned about Birame III. Provided nothing happens to this child, my first friend. That's why I have been waiting here for hours. Hours.

At 2:30 p.m. Mwalimwana and the members of his political bureau appear on the platform draped in national colors. Mwalimwana is wearing a Mao suit. His language is simple and direct.

"My children, did we have roads when the white man was here? Hospitals, schools, housing for your parents, state shops for buying rice, oil and tomato sauce? The Lebanese and the Mauritanians would insult your fathers and mothers for ten francs on credit. My children, what is it you reproach your father for? If one of you has a reproach to make, let him stand up and not be afraid. Don't be afraid. If a child washes his hands, he can eat with his elders. Now it's your turn."

Play-acting? Sincere? Does the crowd fall for it? How would I know? I look around me, but I can't read a thing on these faces.

Suddenly, one of the Party women rushes from the side aisle onto the platform, which literally shudders under her weight. She clasps her hands to her head. She shouts. What? I can't understand. Mwalimwana makes a gesture for her to keep quiet. She shouts louder. A carefully rehearsed duet? How would I know? Other women get up in turn and scream. Then turning to the students and pupils she utters a torrent of words which I don't understand. Let's ask a neighbor. I would disturb him.

A pupil gets up and others follow. What are they saying? I can't wait any longer. I lean over.

"Shh!" my neighbor says, exasperated.

Members of the Political Bureau cross the platform and surround Mwalimwana who is standing while applause shakes the hall. I have never attended anything of this sort. I can't understand what is going on. Silence.

Then, guarded by soldiers, the twelve student leaders from the Institute together with Birame III appear on the platform. They are wearing military uniforms. Mwalimwana has decided, once they have repented, to send them for a few months to camps out in the bush to tar the roads, dig the wells for their brothers in the rural communities and learn to respect their elders again.

"A sound decision, Mwalimwana! I like what you do."

"Let them go back to our villages, the city air has turned their heads."

Birame III is there, bundled into his oversized fatigues. He looks so thin! Look at me Birame III and listen. You used to call me your big sister. Admit your mistakes and take the oath. Don't play the hero. Don't be afraid to lose face in front of your friends. They lost it when the soldiers arrived at the Institute. Our history is full of atrocities. It started with those they threw to the sharks, perhaps even earlier. The Oscar for imagination goes to the Americans. They roasted us, dismembered us, tarred us, stuffed us with gunpowder and exploded us in mid-air between heaven and earth. They wore white masks to remove the genitals with silver tongs. Not that the Europeans were any better. They made us into cannon fodder. Don't add to the list of atrocities. Your drop is useless in an ocean of blood. What matters, Birame III, is to live. Never mind how. Birame, can you hear? One by one the students come forward to the yells of the women. They rub their hands together, against their cheeks, then palms turned upwards, take the oath. After each oath the audience repeats: "Amin."

Birame III is the last in the line. He runs his beautiful slit eyes over the room. Don't play the fool, Birame. We're all with you here. Intelligence is often self-denial. Afterwards, I'll give you whatever you want: a childhood. Perhaps mine would have suited you after all. He comes forward, he takes the microphone in his hands and suddenly, as if seized with folly, shouts:

"Never, never. They have betrayed the revolution. Never, never."

Then he jumps from the platform. The students and pupils stand up. But the Party women have already got him. The soldiers drag him away shouting: "Never! Never!" And that's that! Birame III is too hard-headed, too stubborn. They were right. They know him better than I do. Mwalimwana gets up. The national anthem. The platform is cleared.

Now what's going to happen? The crowd gradually thins out. I look for a familiar face. Where is Saliou? He must be somewhere. The Mercedes leave, standards flying. What are they going to do with this child?

I'm not going to start to cry in the middle of the street. If I cry, they'll come up, commiserating and surprised.

"Woman, why are you crying? Have you lost your husband, your father, your child? Woman, you've got good clothes, good shoes and you're crying?"

I have to admit, I'm lost. They have their problems that I can no longer ignore. I need a guide, an interpreter, a chief linguist to make offerings and have the message from the oracle decoded. What am I going to do until this evening? Go to Saliou's? They'll talk about Birame III. And for the time being, I don't want to think about Birame III. Shouldn't I think about myself first?

What I need is a double scotch or a man. As the second is unlikely to appear, let's go for the whiskey.

Jean Lefevre and Adama greet me with shouts of joy. Adama has a small bout of malaria. She is wrapped in three cloths. Do they know what's going on in town? Jean Lefevre shrugs his shoulders.

"Student agitation? It's chronic. They don't know what they want."

It's obvious he doesn't care either. All that matters is Rouen. As soon as he has slaved enough in this hole, he'll go back and buy a hotel. Naturally, Adama will go with him. And they'll talk of an Africa as green and leafy as a Douanier Rousseau.

To tell the truth I wouldn't think twice about all this if it concerned some anonymous student. One of those adolescents dragging his feet across the Institute's yard holding the little red book. But Birame III! I never took him seriously. I half listened to his lucubrations on China that sets the example, etc. I realize now. They were not lucubrations. They were convictions, beliefs, an ideal for which he had the courage to defy Mwalimwana and the soldiers. He was so small on the platform, so thin!

That's another blow fate has dealt me. It would have to be him! What do you think they'll do to him now?

"They'll mess him up a bit. They have their methods. Don't get mixed up in it. Stop thinking about it, Veronica."

It's all very easy to say. Wouldn't I do better to book my seat on the next DC-10 out of here? I feel it, I'm going to be dragged into it, mixed up in an adventure for which I am not at all prepared . . . not at all. My problems are quite different. And don't tell me they're more futile. They have poisoned my life. Poisoned, yes! But I was in no risk of losing it.

Birame III will manage. With the help of the whiskey I feel better. Jean Lefevre is talking of Rouen. His parents had a paint shop. He grew up with the smell of paint. Almost forty and it still makes him sick. Not really the smell. The memories that go with it. I'm not the only one whose childhood is difficult to digest. The solution would no doubt be to forget them. Draw a line. I can't. Even now I can see them.

"What's she doing in Africa? She never knew what she wanted."

They've got me prisoner. Just when I think I'm a long way off, I am really very close. And that's the worst of it. Even if they died, I wouldn't be rid of them. The whiskey has helped, I'm sure. I don't exactly see life through rose-colored glasses. But even so. I can go home and face the oncoming night. I must say I'm beginning to get fed up with this dump. Time drags. Time is a monster with a neck bloated with blood. If you twist it, you're blinded like Bakari Dian when he killed Bilissi.

I'll never go back to Segou.

For people to see me in this state.

I read. What do you expect me to do? I'm reading the Mandingo epics. When you think of it, that too is part of my therapy. Perhaps these ancestors were mine and I'm not a bastard. Let's read. Try and read.

Am I that good at making my wishes come true? Ibrahima Sory is standing in front of me. I would almost take him for a ghost. Silamaka raised from the dead. Does Ibrahima Sory exist? Or is he a figment of my imagination? Of my frustration? He smiles at me in the shadow. Do ghosts smile?

"I have to go and inspect a camp at Samiana. Would you like to come with me?"

A military camp! What a setting for a love tryst! If it is love after all.

"You haven't left town yet. Samiana is a lovely region on the edge of the lagoon."

My hesitation is over in a flash. Who would throw the first stone? Quite a few. So what!

The god at last deigns to droop an eyelid. The road is straight. The vegetation stripped by the dry season has a certain charm about it. The huts are round under their straw roofs.

He doesn't say a word. Perhaps that fascinates me as well. The weight of his silence. I grew up in the midst of howler monkeys. Witty repartee was a must. Nig-wits. Ha, ha!

Not a word. Children mistake the Mercedes and sing the standard "Mwalimwana, Mwalimwana!"

How many miles? Fifty or five hundred? The driver hurries to open the door for me. Soldiers are holding hurricane lamps over their heads. The night is black. I enter the house of Duma.

Two men are sitting inside, which brings me down to earth. One of them is in military uniform. The other in a ceremonial boubou. They stare at me and I can see in their eyes that intrigued sense of lust two males have in the presence of a third man's bedmate. Let's come back to earth. It all boils down to sex. Introductions. Greetings.

"There's not much for dinner. If we knew Ibrahima Sory was bringing such a charming visitor . . . "

"But he's always been a dark horse."

They laugh. Merely sex? Not for me. In that case, it would be so much easier. Everyone knows you get tired of sex quickly. It's when the mind, the imagination starts to work. I got it into my head that this man would reconcile my two selves. And consequently, them. And us. That I would at last be at peace. If only these two intruders would leave.

But no, they laugh, they talk and drink mint tea. I am half stretched out on the sofa. I have no idea what they're talking about. One of them, not Ibrahima Sory, turns to me.

"You should learn Fulani."

First Mande, now it's Fulani. In other words, you need to be polygot in this country!

Won't they ever go away? At last they get up. They pay their farewells. They disappear into the night. At last!

In my opinion it's not the first time you make love, but the second, that is the most delicate. You are no longer strangers, eager to get to know each other. Not yet intimate enough to stop at nothing. I remain lying on the sofa, not knowing what to do with myself. In the present situation the ritual (or anti-ritual) which I am used to is not applicable. He blows out the hurricane lamp and all is darkness. Don't you ever speak to the women in your bed?

He laughs in the dark.

"Is it really the moment?"

But it has always been recognized from time immemorial that pillows are a place for confidences. True, some have nothing to confide. Individuals, sound in mind and body, do exist. So he doesn't want to know who I am, where I come from, what I've come to do so far from home? If he's not interested, if he doesn't ask, how can I call up my rab so that they leave me alone?

He must help me find a cure. My hatred, my contempt. My explanations must be sincere—not like those patients who continue to lie to their psychiatrist. This contempt they managed to engrave on me. That's the worst of it. Celia Theodonos arrived in the first form. A hard-working girl, straight from Grands Fonds Cacao in her faded print dress. There was already derisive laughter at the mention of her place of birth. To the question, father's profession, she replied in a low, trembling voice: small farmer. She was our Char' Bovari. I was as bad as the others. What became of her? We made her our scapegoat. We called her Topsy. I was as bad as the others. At the same time, by a strange sense of perversion, I wanted her to hit back or stand up to our insults. She couldn't. She thought she could disarm us by flattery. Me as well as the others. I hate them, but behave just like them. Exactly the same.

Say something man. It's whores I believe that are screwed in silence. If you don't say something, this wild ploughing back and forth will only satisfy my body. He's thoughtful, this man. He asks me politely:

"Tired?"

Don't worry. We can begin again and again. I'll never say enough. Not yet . . . He sighs with contentment and moves to one side.

"Why did you come to Africa?"

Ah, at last . . . Be careful not to discourage him by pouring out all my problems in one go. It's been some time since I've been dying to make a confession. Let's try and be relaxed.

I was fed up. I was living in Paris. With a white man.

"With a white man?"

Really quite shocked. Yes, yes. Let me go on. I wanted to escape from the family, the Mandingo marabout, my mother, the black bourgeoisie that made me, with its talk of glorifying the Race and its terrified conviction of its inferiority. And then gradually I came round to thinking that this form of escape was not valid, that it was hiding something else. I could have escaped in the other direction. Make up for the distance they had lost. Put down roots within myself. Do you understand?

"In other words, you have an identity problem?"

The tone is somewhat mocking . . . Is that it? Perhaps I'm not making myself clear.

"There was a young black American girl here who had the same sort of problem, I believe. She ended up having her hair plaited like our women and having herself renamed Salamata."

What an amusing story! How it amuses him. I can imagine this poor Shirley alienated by white America and trying to cure herself. Amidst their laughter. Perhaps you made love to her? Perhaps you're the specialist for neurotics from the Diaspora? We are after all the Diaspora! He laughs louder.

"Oh no! My weak point is pretty women. And in the name of Allah she was very ugly!"

Yes, just a question of sex.

I feel tired, disheartened. I'm no longer in the mood for

confidences. I close the big studded trunk with Mabo Julie's dress, her Sunday felt-embroidered slippers, the silk kimono belonging to the Mandingo marabout, sitting down for an English breakfast. What's the point? It's not worth a damn to him. He speaks to me like a sick or else a very stupid child.

"Go to sleep. And stop dramatizing for nothing."

I can assure you, I never realized the rank of Ibrahima Sory or I never wanted to before seeing him in the hut at Samiana, dressed in military uniform. A kind of paratrooper's dress with lots of buttoned-down pockets and a cap. It's as if I have discovered his link with the fate of Birame III. As if I saw him drag him from the Party Headquarters far from the Party hags.

In the poetry of the night I hadn't seen this grey wall and the camp buildings flying a dirty flag. In the early morning, I feel sick.

Ibrahima Sory is talking with his two colleagues of yesterday, both in military uniform. They are serious, aloof, indifferent. The warrior's rest is over. They move off in a dark green jeep. What am I going to do with myself?

The young soldier who is anxiously looking at me is no doubt responsible for satisfying my whims. Why does he seem frightened to death of me? Because I go to bed with his boss? If only he knew how little it all means.

Yes, a question of sex.

He executes and drives me to the lagoon.

Flat, lifeless, grey like the sky. There must be a certain beauty in this landscape. Like a taste of death. You feel the spirits prowling at ground level or sitting in the branches of the baobabs. Like my rab who won't go back to the Sangomar point.

Is there a legend attached to the lagoon? My companion doesn't know and apologizes in his way.

"I'm from the North."

Like the Minister? His face lights up.

"From the same village."

Does he like being a soldier? To which he quietly replies: "There's a lot of unemployment around."

I've had dates in my time. Not to mention those when I was sixteen. When we came down on our bicycles. Aunt Paula had given

me a key. There was a Cayenne rose bush right under the window.
And on the bedroom wall, a picture of Christ, his heart pierced with a
kind of dagger. Aunt Paula was a great churchgoer and never missed
a mass. She thought it right for me to take communion every Sunday
between mother and father. I took communion piously. Sometimes at
the foot of the altar we bumped into the de Rosevals. Not Jean-
Marie. He no longer set foot inside church to the despair of his
mother. I would have liked to have had his courage. No, Sunday after
Sunday, I swallowed my round wafer. That's what shocked my
mother the most. She cried.

"You were in a state of mortal sin! Mortal sin!"

What would have happened if I had been pregnant? Mme de
Roseval said she would kill her son with her own hands rather than
see him marry a negress. Same black bourgeoisie! Thank goodness
my womb was already sterile.

I've had some dates, but none of them like this one. The young
soldier suggests we continue as far as the village. We arrive at a well
dug in the center of a square of mud huts. Nobody. Some girls are
drawing water in black, rubber water skins. How do they live in a
village like this? What is life like in these surroundings? Surprise! The
garage *cum* bar is owned by a white man. One of the last colonials.
Those whom nothing will budge from Africa—neither the specter of
communism, nor the the threat of nationalization or foreign currency
controls. He stinks of whiskey and decadence.

"Where are you from?"

Is it that obvious that I'm not from here? Will I end up plaiting my
hair as well and renaming myself Salamata to try and merge with the
crowd?

The young soldier watches me in horror as I drink up a glass of
beer. How does he see me? Perhaps it would help if I knew. The
Frenchman is from Montauban.

"Nothing left! No family. No friends."

And me?

We return to camp. The jeep bumps along on the ruts in the
road. We pass men with conical-shaped hats riding donkeys. They
move over in fright as the car goes by. Their hats hide their faces.
Why am I here? The sun is immobile. Why?

I came to seek a land inhabited by Blacks, not Negroes, even spiritual ones. In other words, I'm looking for what remains of the past. I'm not interested in the present. Beyond that, I am seeking the Oba's palace, the carving on their masks and the songs of the griots. An absurd undertaking? No worse than a man crossing the Sahara who can't help imagining what it was like before its desertification.

We arrive at the hut. It's deserted. Don't be fooled, this hut is luxurious. In the center, wide and circular, like a tree trunk, is a wooden column carved with caymans, calaos and panthers supporting the roof high above our heads. Animal skins cover the floor as well as strange, attractive furnishings. The young soldier explains that they come from the army workshops using traditional techniques.

I've had other dates in less luxurious surroundings. Where it was more fun. Time drags.

I'll never go back to Segou.

For them to see me in this state.

Ibrahima Sory re-emerges, regal, yet military in his jeep. He springs down. This man has the quality I prize most in others, probably because I lack it so terribly. He's at ease with himself. His skin, rubbed since childhood with shea butter, fits him like a glove.

"What did you do with yourself?"

What did I do?

"You're disappointed with Africa, aren't you? It's not at all what you imagined in the Latin Quarter!"

What I imagined? What did I imagine? A friend of the Mandingo marabout had been a colonial administrator in French West Africa, as it was then called. Another one who had done the Race proud. You should have seen him! He brought back ostrich eggs, elephant tusks and a way of speaking to the servants that put everybody at ease. The local press gave wide coverage to his visits to the island. His vision had no influence on me; as he had bad breath I always used to hide whenever he came. Actually, I never imagined anything. A great black hole. The Dark Continent.

Two

The news of Saliou's dismissal hits me like a ton of bricks. I arrive out of the blue from my somewhat unsuccessful tryst in Samiana. And wham! My expatriate colleagues are surprised by my amazement and revolt.

"Since he couldn't keep order at the Institute . . . "

So they think it's quite normal? To deprive a man of his livelihood overnight? Saliou dismissed! Another trick fate has played on me. Yes *me*. As if he absolutely wanted me to feel concerned and step down into the arena with the gladiators. Saliou!

The new director of the Institute is wearing a Mao suit. It's obvious he is the iron hand without the velvet glove. There's no danger with him of order not being kept. Law and order! He summons the teachers to an amphitheater . . . :

"I need your cooperation."

Not mine! I didn't come here to keep law and order. The police and the soldiers are there for that! Saliou dismissed! I slip out of the amphitheater. The students are lining up in front of the laundry. They're going to be made to wear Mao caps. No more slapdash. And jump to it! The revolution starts with new clothes. A little while back I was surprised at discovering the expatriates' hostility towards Saliou. They called him a demagogue, accused him of systematically favoring students versus teachers, of fostering indiscipline and a spirit of revolt. Is it true? I'm like a horse with blinders in all this.

I step over the cripples at the entrance to the Institute and wake up the taxi driver who is asleep.

Saliou's house is full of people. The news of his dismissal has spread and misfortune, like good fortune, is something to be shared. Life is a sad merry-go-round. In power one day, disinherited the next. Allah, pity! I recognize Birame III's guardian. He is accompanied by a skeleton of a man dressed in a dark brown boubou the color of his skin. He takes my hands in his as if he were going to kiss them. Birame III had spoken of me in his letters home. He called me little mother. No, I'm not going to cry. Cry in shame. If I cried they would look at each other compassionately.

"She really loves us. She's one of us."

Whereas it's not true. Yesterday, only yesterday . . .

Saliou is in the children's room sitting between two cradles. He is alone. He looks sad and despondent. He stares at me. I'm frightened. I feel as if I'm being x-rayed. Lung, liver, heart and intestines get the treatment. It's ridiculous, he can't know anything. Yet the desire to confess everything is heartrending. Saliou, listen, and try to understand. This man is the remedy I came to seek. I know he'll reconcile me with them, with us, with myself. My thoughts get mixed up. They lose all meaning.

"I drove Birame III's father over to see you yesterday. Where were you?"

Where was I?

I was wandering in the bush like those ancestors looking for a grandson to be reincarnated. I was sitting on the lower branches of a baobab, whistling eerily at passers-by. Sometimes I tried to drink their blood.

"We know for certain they have killed him."

They beat him to death. Oh, they'll say it was an accident. Who? Who?

Saliou, don't be ridiculous! Don't ramble! Don't be melodramatic; it's such poor taste.

"They'll say it's an accident. We'll know it's an assassination."

I'd laugh if I had the strength to. But it's impossible. I look at him with terror, for supposing it's true.

It's this impression of a nasty trick that's haunting me. If only it had happened to someone else. Like those catastrophes you read about in the newspaper. Those scenes on television. Plane crash in Chile—seventeen dead. You have to admit it, the bodies are a long way off. They don't stop you from drinking your tea in the morning. Sometimes you're even sipping a whiskey while they count them.

Birame III!

"We are certain . . . "

Certain? Me too. I can be certain. I can make inquiries. And right from the very source!

"Veronica . . . "

Perhaps I had never looked at the town until then. As I said, I started to like it, a little like my love for Mabo Julie when I was a child. Without ever thinking she suffered from being so ugly. One day, I must have been over thirteen, I was sitting in the kitchen. She was chopping up chives very thinly and I asked her:

"Why didn't you ever get married?"

She laughed and shook her head, which fifteen years later fills me with sorrow, as I realize all the despair there was in this gesture.

"Get married! Who'd want a wicked old nigger woman like me?"

"Would you have liked to have gotten married?"

"I'd have liked to have had children."

"Aren't I one of them?"

She laughed again.

"Oh, God is kind. He didn't make you the child of poor old Julie Boisgris."

That's what the town and country are to me. An environment, a context whose very nakedness suits my mood. And suddenly I feel like stopping men, women and children and shouting:

"Who are you? What do you want? Are you happy? Happy—happy."

What would they say?

There is a crowd in front of the radio station. Women on their way to market have set down their enamel basins.

"A thief, there's a thief gone inside."

A poor devil who can hardly walk emerges from the radio station between two robust police officers. The crowd lets them through. The women keep murmuring. What are they saying? They are praying he's not made to suffer too much. He too came out of a woman's womb.

"We all came out of a woman's womb."

Them, me, all of us!

I had never dreamt of going to the Ministry for the Defense and the Interior. It's an enormous building, not far from the U.S. embassy. I enter a room where two guards are crunching kola nuts, while a third dozes near a phone. I don't know what sort of expression I have, but they stand up startled and come to attention. Mr. Minister, Mr. Minister. Oh, no dilly-dallying, I have to see him. *I have to.* Despite his powers of self-control that I have already noted, Ibrahima Sory seems taken aback at seeing me. He arches his brows.

"Who is Birame III?"

Oh no, Mr. Minister, the town, the whole country is ringing with the name and you claim it's the first time you've heard it. I'm told the students have composed a song in his honor. It's not broadcast on the national radio, of course. But everybody's humming it.

He still had the taste of milk
In his mouth
But he shouted NO
NO to the soldiers
NO to the tyrant.

A student?

He gets up. I am always surprised when he stands up that he is no more than average height. Hardly taller than I am. He gives me such an impression of force and weight.

"Veronica, don't think your relation with me will protect you. If you're to be struck down, I'll do nothing to prevent it."

Struck down? Why would I be struck down? Who would? I'm just a foreigner in a mess.

"This affair is Mwalimwana's concern. I've got better things to do, believe me, than to look after spoiled, impertinent and stubborn students."

Spoiled! Birame III! He used to wash in the open in his guardian's yard, rub himself with a handful of straw and dry himself with a cloth. Spoiled! He shrugs his shoulders and looks at me as if I suddenly amuse him.

"One piece of advice. Don't get mixed up taking sides. This country isn't yours. You don't understand anything. We have our methods."

I suppose assassination is your favorite method? He laughs, a very young-sounding laugh, relaxed.

I must say, he's right in a way. I sounded ridiculous.

Who rushed me into this role which does not fit me at all? The role of judge. Justice varies according to time and place. Don't I know that? I sit down in a leather armchair. He leans over me and suddenly seems kind, almost fraternal.

"I'll have you driven back to Heremakhonon."

To Heremakhonon! The assassin always returns to the place of the crime. Now, now, don't be melodramatic. Melodramatic? It's truer than fiction. NO, no, no. The whole affair was conceived by Saliou's overpowered brain. Proof, you need proof in such cases. Perhaps Birame III simply left for the North with his comrades. He's just arrived! The villagers are emerging from their umbrella-roofed round huts. The sheep are bleating between the cows' feet. The women, whispering:

"He's a child from the coast."

To Heremakhonon! Yes, at least they won't get me there. Them. I mean Saliou, the guardian, Birame III's father, the cripples from the market and the two whitish lepers who sell baskets around the mosque. In actual fact I've two packs of dogs on my heels. The family whom I've been dragging around for years, and a new one, brand new, whose bite I haven't yet assessed. Just think how ridiculous it is! I came reaching for peace and what did I find? A corpse. I have never lost anybody I loved. Except Mabo Julie. I was sixteen. For years she complained of pains in her stomach. Occasionally, Dr. Carzavel, first black doctor, who treated my mother's hay fever, would feel around her navel with his fingers.

"Julie, you'll outlive us all!"

Then he would close his bag and pinch my cheek on the stairs. One day, there was Mabo Julie spurting blood. Literally. They took her to the clinic. They opened her up. Malignant tumor. She died.

Oh, she had a lovely funeral, the Mercier's servant. It gave Marthe, my mother, the occasion to parade around the gardens of the Sous-Prefecture in her lace dress. The Mandingo marabout sniffed.

"She ended up being one of the family."

I had dry eyes . . . I never knew how to cry, just like now.

The gardener at Heremakhonon is a Fon from Dahomey whose search for a job brought him as far as this place. He was in the war in Indochina. Had been a docker at Marseilles. A lorry driver in Algeria. He talks to himself, a bit of French, a bit of English, a bit of Arabic under his conical hat. Sometimes he stops to mime an imaginary combat. Or laugh out loud. In his wanderings he has learned to read and he carries around in his pocket a dog-eared, abridged copy of *Les Miserables*. Abdoulaye says he's a sorcerer. He shouts to me from behind his hedge of roses.

"Mademoiselle, life is how you want it?"

No, Agossou. Life is a bitch with a bum leg. She smokes a pipe and sits on the doorstep of her hut, and when I'm within reach, she mutters wickedly. She has cast a spell on me and I cannot rid myself of it. That's why I'm wandering from one continent to another, looking for my identity, dixit Ibrahima Sory, and finding bodies in my path.

In any case, I shall have to confess. Yet another confession. Yet another sin. Venial or mortal?

The priest has the breasts of a woman. He got a litter of kids off a one-eyed negress called Délices who lives at the entrance to Carénage. Don't his superiors know? The Mandingo marabout, who claims to be a Voltairian (can you imagine that?), is certain they know, but they're just as bad. And naturally it sickens me to have to tell him.

"I ate my sister's share of cake that she left in the kitchen."

Later, I made up for it. When I had mortal sins by the dozen and the worst of all (right?) the sin of the flesh. I mumbled:

"That's all, Father!"

"Well, my child. Say your rosary a dozen times. May God give you the force to keep you this pure."

And I swallowed my wafer.

Confess to Saliou. Grope for his hand in the shadows, so as not to see his eyes. My whole life I have gotten into impossible situations. Impossible? Why? What business have I with them? Abdoulaye is worried seeing me sitting motionless in this striped armchair. He would like to see me capricious, demanding, agitated, to have the pleasure of serving and satisfying me. Perhaps not the pleasure. Well, that's his role. What's mine?

I need a good night's sleep. Sleep is a close relative to death. For years it carried me off to India. To the Taj Mahal. It even took the breath of the English away. I imagined myself a Brahmin's daughter (not an untouchable's of course) with a tilaka in the middle of my forehead. And then my sleep got worse. Until the intrusion of the street cleaner. Final intrusion. Last act. The baggage is ready. We're going to take our chattels elsewhere. That's how we turned up without baggage, without a guide in an unknown country. I was parachuted into the Sahel. All around me, animal carcasses.

To please Abdoulaye, I'll drink some mint tea. He is sitting cross-legged at my feet, and there is this little sound of running water. Shall I ask him a question? On what? Better close my eyes. May the peace of God be with me.

I couldn't tell you when Ibrahima Sory came back and if I had waited a long time. There he is on the terrace, half joking, half in politeness:

"Have you calmed down?"

Abdoulaye leans over to say a few words. He waves him away impatiently. Abdoulaye disappears. Understood, it's time to rest. I am the warrior's rest. Yet I come from an island where the women are solid matrons. You somehow have to make up for the males backing out—three centuries have made our men fathers and little else. They procreate like ploughmen sowing their seed by mistake in the first field they fall upon. When I say women, however, I don't mean those of my milieu. No, not those. They've realized that a real woman must have hay fever, allergies, and in short be the weaker sex. Their force is disproportionate to their social status. The *nec plus ultra* was Dr. Carzavel's wife who went from church to her rest bed. But who gave birth, year in, year out, proof that from the reproduction angle she wasn't doing too badly.

"I have made inquiries about your student. He went to the North with his friends. He'll tarmac the roads and clear the forests. It'll give him time to think."

Think about what? What do you expect Birame III to think about? He shuts his eyes.

"Women tire you out. That's why I live 600 miles away from mine."

From his? It's all very well saying one is broad-minded. He's married then?

"I was married while a student in Paris to a young girl whom I saw twice when I was studying the Koran at her father's, a holy marabout."

And where is she? What is she doing, this wife?

"In the North. Her compound is the finest in the village. She has two sons in good health. She's happy."

Yes, happiness, like justice, is a relative concept. And him? Is he happy? He laughs openly. This man does have a lot of fun in my company.

"Me! I leave the pursuit of happiness to Westerners. I've got other problems."

Such as?

"Rebuilding a country that colonialism has drained of its strength."

Rebuilding? By imprisoning students?

He laughs louder.

"Veronica, you wouldn't be one of those left-wingers who have decided to make Africa their battleground?"

I defend myself. Oh, how I defend myself. Now I know what I wanted to know. Birame III is alive. He's tarring roads in outsized dungarees. He'll come back to us later on with blisters on his hands.

"Do you know what I'd do if I had the choice? I'd retire to my village, I'd pray and meditate over the Koran."

Really? Excuse me, Mr. Minister, you don't look like a mystic. Nor do you behave quite like one. You may be perhaps one after all. Once again it's the West that sets the flesh apart from the spirit. Perhaps making love is your way of paying homage to the Creator. Woman is a field and man her ploughman. Plough me, ploughman. I understand him better each time—love for him is a game, an amusement, a sport. He throws himself in body and soul and then doesn't think anymore about it. And where do I come in? Screwed, literally and figuratively. If he doesn't love me, if he doesn't let me love him, how can I return to my womb? How can I be born again? Free of shame and hidden contempt? He has to help me. Put a name to my rab so that they leave me and return to the Sangomar point.

He moves over. I'm used to his courtesy question, so unexpected. I shake my head. We're off again. At top speed, down the mountain slope.

The hour of confession came more quickly than I thought and not at all as I expected. I had imagined an interview in the shadows, conducive to self-reproach, whispering and hesitant. Instead of that, full daylight and Saliou pulling me out of my siesta, shouting: "Tell me it's not true!"

How did he know? I should have suspected it. This town is nothing but an overgrown village. Nothing remains a secret.

"Tell me it's not true!"

His thin, bony fingers dig into my shoulder. Saliou, let's stay calm. Let me explain.

"What is there to explain? Don't you know who Ibrahima Sory is? Haven't Birame III and myself told you enough about him? The most reactionary and retrograde element among Mwalimwana's associates. Because of his name, his family, he enjoys unwarranted influence. Unwarranted. We studied together in Paris. He used to parade around in the midst of a court of young ladies from the upper crust excited at the idea of making love to a black prince . . . "

Saliou, Saliou, that's how I feel.

"Each setback, each blow to the revolution, he's behind it . . . What did you want to explain to me?"

Obviously, when the question is posed point blank my ideas get mixed up. Wait! I'm convinced. On what grounds? I don't know. Let's go on. I'm convinced he can save me. Reconcile me with myself, in other words my race or rather my people.

"Him? Him? It was the blood of the people that got his family rich."

Somewhere we are mixing our references and any dialogue is impossible. For him, the people are an exact, concrete notion. For me . . . I sit down in an armchair since he has loosened his grip. We look at each other across the room. He looks as though he's suffering. Because of me?

"Why Veronica?"

What can I say to that? He can't understand. He would have had to live my life.

"So many men in this country. Of all the serious, reliable comrades you go and choose this one."

He suddenly turns presumptuous. He wants to enroll me, recruit me. Right down to the person I make love to. In a way he's no different from the Mandingo marabout. I don't have the heart to be unpleasant to him. One of my first two friends is tarring roads. Am I going to lose the other? He shakes his head.

"I haven't given up making you see the light."

Where there's hope . . . they say. I don't believe it. If there were no hope, if the days were taken for what they are worth, everything would be different. No more dupes!

The rough voice of the muezzin can be heard. The small talk must end. I have a lecture to give. That's what I'm paid for. That's why I'm here. Nothing else matters.

The students are dragging their heels around the room. Some of them are ostentatiously smoking. It is forbidden to smoke inside the Institute. It doesn't bother me. I'd give these kids cigarettes if I could. Not those manufactured by the local Chinese-built factory. But Virginia tobacco. Benson and Hedges. The symbol of your success. Now you've hung about long enough. Into class. I give the example.

On the blackboard in red chalk spelled out in capitals: WE SHALL DESTROY THE MINISTERS, THEIR MERCEDES AND THEIR WHORES.

Is that me? I turn round. No doubt about it, that's me. They are at the entrance to the room, their hands in the pockets of their brand new Mao tunics. They are looking at me. Hostility, contempt. Contempt yet again. Contempt flowers under my feet. What am I to do? They watch me.

First, feelings of hostility. Turn around and thunder: "Who wrote that?" and make for the Director's office. Make a case for Order, Discipline and Respect for the teacher. Trigger off my little act of repression. They are playing on velvet. They know I won't do anything. That I'm a down-and-out traveller. That they can make a surprise attack. Leave me covered in blood in the streets. I'm not going to burst into tears. They're watching me. An adult should never lose face. That I guessed from childhood. The sponge is big, square and green like an unwholesome piece of seaweed. It wets my hand. I wipe off the board. Minister's whore? What right have they to judge me? Are they going to shave my head? Will they hang me from the branches of a tree? My body will rot amid the blossoms of the flame tree.

What right? If I understand correctly making love in this country comes down to making a political choice. I wipe my chalky hands on my handkerchief. I turn around. They are coming in. I would like them to do something violent. Spit in my face for instance as they each go by. It would be very Bunuel. Thick, frothy gobs of spit like during Ramadan. What would I do then? Nobody is spat upon without reacting. Instead of that they sit down and look at me. They wait. What for? I start my class with a steady voice. There's no doubt about it, I've got a level head now. Not like the first time or even the second.

The Caribbean Festival. Chateau de Vincennes. Whatever came over me? Nine years, I'm telling you. Homesickness.

They were standing at the entrance, their black berets tilted to one side. All that was missing were the rifles. Jean-Michel doesn't understand creole. I do. I did learn it after all and haven't forgotten it. Their insults, half out loud, between their teeth, drilled into my flesh. What did I do? Well, I decamped. Jean-Michel didn't understand a thing.

"So capricious!"

Capricious? Those young things would have lynched me if they could. First me. Perhaps you later. Yes, I'm more level-headed now. I don't back out. I give my class. Right to the end.

"Mademoiselle, I swear we didn't want to. It was Oumar . . . "

You didn't want to, but you let him do it. It's always the same. The silent majority only emerges from their silence once the bombardment is over. The country in ruins. And the orphaned children running in the ditches. Then they say they have had enough of all this blood as well.

"We didn't want to, I swear. We wanted to stop him."

Let's forget about it, Abdou. After all, it is my private life. Do you know what that means? Abdou was Birame III's best friend and just as puny and dirty with a guardian who had little time to look after him. I gave him a boubou, a pair of shoes and exercise books, just like Birame III. Not that I'm boasting about it. It just calms my conscience. Doesn't solve their problems I know. He follows me across the yard. Why does he stick to me so? Is he afraid of having killed the goose that lays the golden eggs? And how! Since it seems she is under the wing of a minister. Get rid of such evil thoughts. And this child half in tears. The new director is parading in front of his office.

"Well, Mademoiselle, is everything alright?"

He does have a sense of humor! If I told him: "Your darling students have just called me a whore." What would he do? There are some insults which are only washed off in private.

"Collaborate in maintaining order and discipline."

Me, a whore? Who has never received a penny!

If they knew they'd laugh! The Mandingo marabout would hold his sides.

"I am asking all the teachers . . . "

What is he asking? I don't want to be asked anything!

The god at last deigns to drop an eyelid. The gentlest hour of the day. Night is already looming and ready to fall. I hail a taxi whose driver doesn't hear me, deafened by his clapped-out engine. Another stops and smiles.

"Where are you going?"

Where? To find my sister in whoredom. Birds of a feather . . . Adama is emerging from her long siesta. She has just washed, perfumed and combed herself. Jean Lefevre is bawling out an undernourished worker who has spoiled some cement. The two of them shout for joy. Don't tell me they are not trustworthy. You get the confessor you deserve. What can a whore afford except a priest? Or another whore?

I cry a lot. They get worked up.

"What did they do to you? They're evil in this country. All bastards! The whiteman's lash, that's what they need!"

I admit it's ridiculous crying like that. But it has been a rough day. I sniff. I don't feel like explaining the whole business. I merely ask a question. Why is it that no matter what I do they throw stones at me? They try to destroy me?

"What's she saying? Mamadou, a glass of water!"

No, I don't have sunstroke. The sun, which scorches even the subsoil, has not attacked my brain. I want to know why, without fail, my conduct is to blame. With Jean-Marie—I was called Marilisse. With Jean-Michel, too—especially Jean-Michel. And what's more they could say that his brothers were shooting us in the back in Manhattan, creating Bantustans and letting us roast in Aubervilliers. OK, that I can admit. And that's why I left after all. But now what? What are they going to invent now to stop me from making love in peace? Jean Lefevre has opened a bottle of pastis. I drink. Don't I know already what they've cooked up? What they're blaming me for?

"I've always wondered why you came to this hole."

How they'd laugh if they could see me! The Mandingo marabout would forget his bouts of gout which Aida and Jalla tell me are keeping him confined to his armchair two days out of five. It's funny how diseases classify men. Some die from kwashiorkor. Easy to say which ones. Others die of syphilis. We also know which ones. Others have gout from overindulging in good food. He would laugh. He wouldn't be wrong. I'm beginning to understand where I went wrong. If I want to come to terms with myself, i.e. with them, i.e. with us, I ought to return home. To my island specks (dixit the general) tossed to the four corners of the Atlantic by Betsy, Flora and other females. *Home.* Back to the obscene caricatures of my childhood. After all, our black bourgeois clique only represents two or three families. And the mulatto set, very little too. There are all the others. What do they do? I don't know. I only know what I've been told about them. At home. Not here, where I'm a foreigner. Where I'm torpedoed into matters of which I know neither head nor tail. *Home!* Nine years since I've been back, as they say. My mother and father are white-haired. When I was fifteen I read in a play by Ben Jonson (I read healthy books; not the *Principles of Marxism-Leninism*) that black people's hair didn't whiten and I was surprised by Mabo Julie's greying temples when she pushed back her madras.

I feel better, however, after my two pastis. Adama invites me to eat her barbecued chicken with lemon and sweet potato chips. A little like Jean-Michel, who seeing me sink into gloom, used to take me out to eat oysters at the Petit Zinc. The waiters knew us. Diners at the other tables looked at us. Don't be mistaken, going out with a negress can have quite an effect. Provided she doesn't look as though she's just stepped out from behind a cash register at a Monoprix department store. If she's a bit of a tart she's still acceptable. Because basically for the silent majority the line is very thin between a negress and sex. What can Jean-Michel be doing at this moment? At home.

The town seems so small, ridiculous! That's where I was born, however, and grew up. They show me the new district, the council flats that have replaced the huts made of soap cartons and corrugated iron; the motorways; the new hotels, and the wildlife park cut in two by an ice-cold river. I am sitting on a big grey rock, sucking my thumb. A dozen men and women are getting off the bus Bienfaisante Providence. They're beating the *gros-ka.* A couple undulates to the bonda and mimics the motions of making love. Mabo Julie is singing her head off.

At the wheel, the Mandingo marabout sighs:

"Soon we won't be able to go out any more. They'll be everywhere."

Let's drink. At this time of day only the pastis is genuine. Genuine. Genuine. The trouble is that this genuineness gives you a hangover. And how! You can't open your eyes without getting hit over the head with a mallet. And your mouth full of chewing gum. Even so, I didn't dream it, that's something. A black hole from the table loaded with barbecued chicken to this bed already damp with sweat. I have to get back to the Institute. Will the writing be on the blackboard again? If it is, what shall I do? Nothing. Teach, as if nothing had happened. I won't even wipe it off. Or else little bits, if I have to write some difficult words.

Abdourahmane is getting worried. I must really look awful.

A blind man with wide-open eyes has taken to begging at my door in the morning. Oh, shoo him away! Watch it! I'm on a slippery slope. A little bit more and it'll turn to hatred. I'm going to start hating this country, its men, women and children. Simply because I don't understand them, because the distance between them and me irritates me and their smiles perhaps hide what brutally came to light yesterday in the students' eyes. If I start hating them as well, what's going to be left? A man spits a long jet of saliva two inches from my right foot. Not on purpose. It's only Ramadan.

Will the writing be on the blackboard?

It's obvious it won't be. Apparently there are to be no classes.

The students are lined up in the yard this time under the supervision of the militia in party-colored belts, and not the soldiers. What is going on now? My expatriate colleagues explain. Fed up by the whole farce. Pamphlets have been found in the desks, the cafeteria and the dormitories. Pamphlets? Yes, with a picture of that student. What student? Young Birame III. With the caption "Martyr of the African Revolution."

I immediately pull up a chair and sit down, my legs feel weak.

But Birame III isn't dead!

"Go and tell them that! They are certain that the soldiers have beaten him to death in the Chaka camp."

The Saliou version seems to be the most popular.

I'm so fed up with all of this. And I'm not the only one. My colleagues are furious.

"Why don't they shut this bloody Institute down and send us all home."

You have to give them their due! Of course it's the almighty CFA franc that makes them cross the oceans and why not? But they'd prefer to work than remain with their arms folded. If only the town offered pleasant facilities! Alas! All bedlam on the loose . . .

What am I going to do with all these hours to kill?

On the verandah there are piles of pale green paper rectangles. An adolescent's face. A caption. The word "martyr." I press on. Just as I'm wondering which way to go, with the sun battering me on the head, a Mercedes draws up level with me. Inside, a woman draped in a gold lamé boubou, a Carita wig, chewing a 10 inch long stick.

"Veronica!"

Shame on me, I didn't recognize her. Ramatoulaye, formerly princess of Belborg. She moves up to make room for me and I'm overpowered by Chanel No. 5. What was going on at the Institute again? Those students! After everything Mwalimwana has done for them! Spoiled! Spoiled! If they had grown up under the white man! When to get your general certificate was quite a performance! Mwalimwana is a saint whose goodness will be his own downfall.

Instead of regimenting his opponents. It's obvious, behind those children there are hidden instigators and they are the ones that have to be punished. Punished severely. Once and for all.

"Starting with my brother-in-law, Saliou. I'm telling you, even if he is my brother-in-law.

Now there's a man who was offered the post of ambassador. In Berlin, East Germany. What does he want, you tell me, what does he want? And he's dragging his wife and children down with him. And Oumou Hawa doesn't want to divorce. Still young and good-looking, she could easily find herself another husband. Provided she doesn't marry a minister. Then she'd always find herself alone in the house with children, relatives and parasites. Oh! The parasites! The extended family is the bane of Africa!"

The Mercedes stops near the market where the chauffeur runs to fetch three boubous she has given to the Malians to embroider, the best in West Africa she says. What a smell this market has. They plan to have a market like Rungis for the Tonga district. One day this town will look nice. She asks me without any ill intention:

"How is Ibrahima Sory? I haven't seen him for a while." (In fact, my affair is an open secret).

Yes, the extended family is the bane of Africa. Besides her five children she has her younger sister's two children to raise and three children of one of her husband's brothers, a good-for-nothing whom they've not succeeded in keeping gainfully employed. Ibrahima Sory has done everything for him. Ibrahima Sory does have a sense of the family. The old father said it. Everyone knows it. When a man has a son like Ibrahima Sory he can die in peace. A strong believer and respectful of traditions. In spite of myself, I'm all ears. It's quite a different portrait from what I've gotten elsewhere. I know from experience that you can get as many portraits as you want of the same person. And in some ways, they'll all look alike.

"Yes, a good son. A good brother . . . "

A good husband? She laughs. A marriage that is decided and arranged by the families even before the children are born never gives good results. Fortunately, the custom is disappearing. Mwalimwana has launched an all-out campaign against forced marriages. He had all the elders against him. Poor Mwalimwana, here

I am starting to pity him. On one side the Birame III's and the Saliou's who want to change everything. With a reign of justice and equality and power to the people. On the other, those who don't want anything to change. Between the two, the people who don't say a word and whose silence is interpreted by both parties. The people don't utter a word. They pray, they beg, they line up at the cooperatives, the dispensaries, they bury their children, they baptize them, all in silence. Ramatoulaye's villa is close to Ibrahima Sory's (not surprising then that she is informed). It has a less hermetic name "Villa Mon Rêve" and has Directoire furnishings. I feel dizzy! It was this style that the Mandingo marabout had a liking for, don't ask me why. Our house then was furnished in Directoire. No accommodation was made for a tropical *laisser-aller*; it was Directoire pure and simple. What a shock! When I was crawling on all fours, I used to knock my head on this very furniture. When I tried to stand up my little fingers used to grip the very same furniture. And Ramatoulaye's children as well! The older ones come home from their boarding school in Lausanne for short holidays, just like we used to. I mean just like Aida, Jalla, our dear little friends and myself used to. I don't want to be accused of losing my head for nothing. They are like us, you see what that means? Because of this furniture and a few children, my grapefruit juice, which I generally like when I'm not trying to drown my thoughts with pastis, has a taste of gall. Somewhere in the villa, a child is practicing scales and I literally feel sick. It is all coming back, everything. The satin-stitch net curtains, the smell of gladioli that my mother used to like and our piano teacher.

"La! La!"

Calm down. I'm sick and see my sickness everywhere. Even so, who am I to limit them to the balaphon and the kora? To stop them from furnishing their interiors with taste. What does that mean? Isn't it precisely in the name of good taste, etiquette and good manners that they made me what I am?

"Hafsa, quick, two Aspros for Mademoiselle. She has a headache."

It's not Aspros I need. But tranquilizers of a special sort. At lunch I'm more relaxed. The table is laid luxuriously. The cutlery is in silver, the glasses of crystal. But the rice is burnt and the sauce tasteless. The Mandingo marabout, now suffering from gout, would never have tolerated such a menu. Hafsa is scolded and replies bitingly that with all the comings and goings of children, parents and so-called relatives this is the tenth time he has cooked this morning. There's nothing left of the sheep slaughtered yesterday. And he will soon have to start plucking chicken for the evening. Even at the Haile Selassie motel on the road to the airport they didn't work so hard. And they were better paid. And they had two days off a week. Ramatoulaye sighs:

"That's how the servants talk to us now. Mwalimwana's a saint, that's for sure. But thinking he was doing the right thing—and it's true there were too many abuses in our old system. My father, for instance, had the say over the lives of hundreds of men— Mwalimwana planted this idea of socialism in the country, of equality between master and slave, and that's what you get. Students who no longer obey their teachers. Marabouts who are called charlatans. Thieves. Criminals who are not afraid of the courts. Mwalimwana now has regrets. He wants to start all over again. He has realized that socialism will kill Africa. Will kill it far more radically than years of colonialism. Yes it will kill it. Despite what they say."

The argument is beyond me. I have nothing to say. In any case, Ramatoulaye couldn't care a damn about what I had to say.

I have only been to Heremakhonon on invitation or, you could say, on orders. The temptation is too great; you only have to push a little gate in the hedge. Agossou is already at work with a green plastic hose in his hand. He gives me a toothless smile. Abdoulaye rushes up. I suppose the master is having his siesta like the rest of the town. They sleep everywhere at this time. The town is inhabited by foetus—cluttering the market, a stinking womb, blocking Independence Square, under the big trees, burdening the wharves. Abdoulaye smiles: the master never takes a siesta. He is in his office. Working.

Well, the affairs of state are in good hands. The master does, however, consent to tear himself away. As I've said, he's a polite man. He comes forward.

"I was just thinking how I'd like to see you . . . "

Happy to hear it.

"Why?"

He smiles. Just as long as he doesn't start laughing. I've spent the morning getting hammered by the sun, feeling sick at his sister's, eating badly at lunch and so on. He is surprised.

"I've been wondering why you are so interested in this affair. What was there between you and this student?"

Here the tone and the look are those of a cop, a super cop. He is ridiculous. What could there be between that youngster and myself? I'm not interested in initiations, if that's what he's thinking of.

"Haven't I given you my word that all these rumors are false? Cooked up by some . . . "

His word, his word! What is his word worth? The gold standard quoted on the Stock Exchange? Or a worthless shell from the Indian Ocean? Who could tell me?

"Can you wait for me? I'll see my collaborators out."

Collaborators who collaborate in what? What do you do when you are Minister for the Defense and the Interior? Even during siesta, the holies of holies.

"I thought you knew already: we assassinate and imprison unfortunate students."

He goes off laughing. I can't stand his laugh. It has that somewhat complacent sound of my father's. Laughs are funny. Some people chortle and cover their mouth with their hand because they have teeth missing. Others trumpet out loud like Louis Armstrong. And this must be avoided at all costs. A laugh has to be studied like a scale. It was one of the first lessons I was taught. The laugh makes the nigger . . .

The Minister takes almost an hour to see his collaborators out. And if I told him outright that I love him. Or else in such an offhand manner that the cliché would be even worse. And besides I don't even know if it's true. Do I love this man or a certain idea I have to have of Africa? When you think about it, it's the same thing. Loving a man is the myth you create around him. Or with him in mind. In my case perhaps it's a bit more serious because the idea I have is so vital and yet so vague, so blurred. What is this idea? That of an Africa, of a black world that Europe did not reduce to a caricature of itself. That might say: "When the West was in a mess, we governed our peoples with wisdom, we created, we innovated." Instead of explaining all that, I find myself saying: Don't let's make love. He asks politely: "Aren't you feeling well?"

It's not that. Simply we've never talked. Of anything. By the glint in his eye, I guess that I'm starting to amuse him again. Oh, come on. Let's make love. Too bad for me and my passion for psychoanalysis!

"Do you know what you haven't understood yet?"

Mr. Minister, sir, there are quite a number of things I haven't understood yet. In fact I haven't understood anything. Not a thing.

"There's no room here for little personal problems, sentimentality, whims. We've just had a revolution . . . "

Oh yes? Some ascertain that it hasn't taken place, your revolution. Or else it was quick to be betrayed . . .

"You speak about things you don't know . . . "

He's right there. but if he explained things, I'm no thicker than anybody else, I'd understand. The annoying thing is that he has no desire to explain. Firstly, because he thinks it's none of my business; I'm a foreigner. But mainly because I'm more interesting sexually than my head or my heart or both. Come on. Let's make love. And jump to it! And jump high! At home there is the story of a negress who had the thrust of coil springs and regularly sent her partners up to the ceiling. I think there is even a biguine written about her.

The Institute is closed for a month. They have added a disciplinary vacation to the break for Ramadan. What that will solve I don't know. My problem is the immediate future; in practical terms, what am I going to do with this freedom? My colleagues talk of taking off with a jeep. No thank you. I'll not drive miles and miles to come face to face with some monkey, antelope, buffalo or hippopotamus. My childhood zoos are enough. They say that the dancers of the forest paint themselves in white clay and walk around on stilts. I've had my fill of dancers! If I could go north. But I can't. So let's not think about it.

Abdourahamane's children are in a circle around me. I have bought them paint boxes. So they're painting. One of them a hut, the other a car. Another a canoe. What will become of these children? The revolution (if ever there was one) does not seem to have changed their father's condition: houseboy—cook—laundryman, same as before. With two wives, one selling roasted peanuts, a stone's throw from the mosque. The other spitting blood. I had to intervene personally to get their elder brothers admitted to school. No room, retorted the director. Around us a sea of children clutching their new slates. On the pavement the bewildered parents who couldn't find a place for their offspring. Poor Mwalimwana, what a weight on his shoulders! Naturally Saliou would tell me that instead of building schools he prefers building up his military camps. Saliou . . .

Speak of the devil. Here he comes across the garden. He looks as though he has slept in his boubou. If God exists, please don't let him talk about Birame III. I couldn't bear it. He looks gloomily ironic.

"I've just got my posting to a bush school. It's obviously a trick that wouldn't fool anybody. They think I'm going to refuse the job so that they can strike me off as a cadre. Disciplinary measure!"

There's no doubt about it, here they don't trifle with discipline.

Affection is a curious thing! I've become attached to this man whom I didn't know two months ago. As I've said, I and my sisters were like Cinderella and her sisters. We never liked each other. Perhaps Jalla, I could have. She had a kind of irreverence, but she never carried it through to its conclusion. Her marriage is a case in point. It was obvious she could not resign herself to putting up with our black bourgeois circle. So she chose Désiré Grandieu, whose father had been foreman at the Magellan factory and had organized the workers' strike in 1946 to demonstrate their opposition to the status of assimilation. Now that assimilation in the West Indies is so obviously a lure, Déodat Grandieu comes over as a visionary. After having given his name to the Cultural Institute, the capital's left-wing municipality (short on local celebrities) recently named a series of council flats on the former Morne Moustique after him. Déodat was killed in an accident leaving his wife Maiva with four young children, so some left-wing party took charge of his orphans. That was how Désiré, the younger and more gifted son, studied law at the University of Zaghreb and made a great to-do setting up practice as a lawyer of the underdog, specializing in political causes. They say he's very good. He's defended students accused of having thrown rotten eggs at de Gaulle during one of his visits. Had civil servants reinstated after accusations of subversion. But apparently it pays to be the defender of the oppressed. During her last stay in Paris, Jalla was sporting a leopardskin coat.

"I went mad! Mad!"

Especially mad in my opinion because how many times a year can she wear it? At the same time she wanted to drag me to meetings at the Palais de la Mutualité on behalf of some oppressed people in Latin America. She called her eldest son Frantz in honor of Fanon. But his education does not seem any different from ours. I'm naturally very badly placed to judge or condemn. I just keep running. Without ever finishing the race.

"What have you been doing with yourself all this time?"

Not very much I must admit. And it will be worse in the days to come.

"Don't you feel like making yourself useful?"

What does he want me to do? Print underground leaflets? Hide them in my brassiere?

"Stop playing the fool!"

He goes on to explain. He has a friend, a doctor, at the PMS Center in Mafanko. Three pediatric consultations per week. Two prenatal visits. For months he has been clamoring for a competent assistant capable of setting up the mothers' maternity card records. You would think it's easy to find, wouldn't you? Alas! The secretaries that the National School trains after a fashion are only intent on working in some ministry in the hope that, God willing, the minister or his private secretary will notice them and . . . . OK Saliou, I've got the message. The ministers are the local versions of Prince Charming. And the administrative building, a sort of Hollywood where the unknown beauties devoid of talent wait to be spotted. Work at the dispensary? Help the overworked doctor while waiting? While waiting for what? Who cares! I like the idea. Saliou seems happy.

"Basically you're a very good person . . . What happened to you is my fault."

He's beginning to loosen up. What happened to me?

"I should have taken you by the hand and guided you."

It gets better and better! You can only guide someone who asks. Otherwise it becomes an intolerable interference. And then guide me where? Into the bed of a militant companion? So that I'm screwed along the same lines? Why not into *his* bed? To make sure the message gets through. Saliou, I ought to be offended; you've never wanted to go to bed with me. Obviously you'd say that adultery is bourgeois. That's not what he answers. He doesn't answer. He keeps looking at me. And my joke, which is not very delicate, I must confess, falls flat. He looks at me and after a while says:

"I like you very much you know."

I can't be in my normal state, as these few words bring tears to my eyes. Yes, I'll work with this doctor! It's been drummed into me since childhood—work is healthy. Idleness is the root of evil. *Quant nèg pas ka travaill, i ka fé quimbois.* When the nigger doesn't work, he casts spells. We were forgetting, however, the unfortunate lot who worked for nothing for two centuries, sweated blood and tears for nothing. I don't agree with Christophe when he proclaims by the grace of Césaire:

"I ask too much of men? But not enough of black men, Madame."

I've read Césaire too like everybody else. I mean like everybody from our world. In my opinion, it's high time they left the niggers in peace, let them dance, get drunk and make love. They've deserved it. What after all are they expected to do? Prove, prove, prove with mind-bending effort that they are as . . . as the whites. He who takes one step backward is the shame of the Race, the Race, the Race. I'm dropping out. I dropped out a long time ago. I don't want to prove anything any more. No, I've never proved anything.

The doctor's name is Yehogul, which shouldn't surprise me, as he is not from here. But from a country further south. He is small, stocky and covered in scars. Not at all the elongated nobility of the men around here.

"Saliou has told me a lot about you."

What is there to tell about me? I'm intrigued. I know what some people say: "Quite mad! Insane! She never knew what she wanted."

What about the others though? What do they say? My colleagues for instance.

"When could you start?"

Saliou answers for me. He's taken charge of the operation, sitting under a blue-eyed Nestlé baby. I'll start the day after tomorrow since today he's taking me to Diamfamani. What's going on in Diamfamani? Nothing. It's a village where one of his aunts lives who keeps him stocked up with chicken, eggs and sour milk. Sounds interesting! I have the choice between following him or going round in circles at home, waiting for my evasive lover to call. Sex object, the female eunuch that you screw when you feel like it and send back, not to her saucepans, but to her state of inactivity. Let's go to Diamfamani.

"How can you love an assassin?"

For heaven's sake Saliou, let's talk about something else. Neutral, indifferent things. About the weather, for instance, like the English. Unfortunately the weather is foreboding. They predict the worst drought in living memory. And following that, famine. Neutral, indifferent subjects don't exist in this country. You are constantly attacked, raped and forced to take part. What am I doing in this hole?

In Paris I'd be admiring Kandinsky in the Swann gallery. If a DC-10 stopped on the road, I swear I'd take it. But there are no DC-10's; men, women and children waiting for the occasional bus, squatting under the baobabs. Sometimes donkeys. The desolation of this place cuts me to the soul. At first, I was not really aware of it. I was so preoccupied with my personal problems. Now, what would they reply to my question:

"Are you happy?"

"Happiness, stranger, what's that? Do you know?"

Me? Of course not! Those who write "Colors of Africa—For our eyes attacked by the grey of our towns—they blur our senses—burst into shouts—into perfume." How do they do it? What do they see that I don't? Lest we not forget, truth is in the eye of the beholder. Not in the thing beheld.

"Have you got your swimming gear? There's a beach over there."

I know their beaches. The sea is heavy, rough and cold. Not like the beaches of my childhood where I dreamed of drowning. I float. I look at the clouds. Mabo Julie is shouting.

"Don't wet your hair. Salt water spoils it, you know that."

Nine years.

Saliou's right. The beach is pretty. The sea is calm set in a bay. But I don't have a swimsuit. He hasn't either. It didn't bother Jean-Marie and me. Once some children caught us by surprise. They didn't seem very shocked. They must have been used to it in their 12 x 9 foot hut. Their sexual education started at home. Not like mine. When I discovered how children were made and that the Mandingo marabout dabbled in this game with Marthe I went down with a temperature of 100. Dr. Carzavel couldn't understand it.

"It's her puberty! Her puberty!"

Let me make myself clear. It wasn't so much the act. It was that the Mandingo marabout who drummed into us dignity, head up, correct dress and manners hadn't invented his own more refined method. Was it merely because the whites, his secret demigods, were content with this obscene method? Well, wasn't this the ideal occasion to outwit them? I can see the comments of the local daily whose editor-in-chief, an honorary primary school teacher, was one of our friends.

"Our distinguished compatriot, Mr. Mercier, whose work and untiring devotion to the cause of the Race are known to everyone, has invented a noble, delicate and simple method of conceiving children, thereby replacing the vulgarity of mother nature. Henceforth we shall leave the sweat of fornication to the niggers of the lower town. To them and the whites."

No, on this point, like on all the rest, he was content to imitate. Imitate.

"Sometimes I tell myself I'm an idiot. That I'd do better to sit back and live."

You said it, Saliou! These short years we spend with our eyes open between two poles of darkness. He has hitched up his boubou over his knees, revealing his dry legs and his socks sagging into his old leather shoes. He is running sand through his fingers.

You know what started all this for me? When I lost my mother. I was twelve. She had been ill for some time. She thought father's second wife had put a fetish on her. She plastered herself with verses from the Koran. And then one day, she was obviously very ill. They tied her into a cloth suspended on a long pole. And then we set off. My father went in front with his brother. Me behind. We walked five miles to get to the hospital. We waited three hours. The nurses passed by without a look. Finally, we saw a doctor. A white man. He cast a glance at my mother and said: "These people always bring me their sick when it's too late." I understood because I went to school.

Obviously the story is touching and can mark a boy. He can imagine after that he has a personal account to settle with poverty, ignorance, superstition and death. So that men no longer die off like dogs. I don't want to be blamed for being what I am after having seen my mother nurse her daily imaginary ills.

"I don't blame you for anything. I'm just wondering how I can make you understand."

Understand? Find my road to Damascus? Saul, Saul. The scales fall from my eyes. And I rush away to buy the little red book. He isn't laughing. It's true my jokes never amuse Saliou.

"Birame III is not enough. For you he was just a youngster and nothing more . . . "

Oh, don't let's talk about Birame III. I've decided to believe Ibrahima Sory.

"Naturally, it's convenient. It avoids your having any remorse. You hide your head in the sand and leave your arse uncovered."

My goodness he's getting vulgar . . . Shall we go on to Diamfamani? He gets up.

Some fishermen hauling their boat onto the sand greet us.

"Salam malaikum."

"Malaikum salam."

"Are you in peace?"

No, of course not. Peace is a luxury commodity, like sugar before Columbus. Diamfamani has half a dozen compounds. Saliou's aunt's is the last on the road to Tenigbé. The aunt is the first wife of a fat man with a shaved head who is asleep in a deckchair and is hurriedly awakened when we arrive. Everybody looks at me out of curiosity. I feel that I shall soon have to say my little piece on my place of origin. Or else Saliou will. The aunt laughs. "She says you ought not to listen to me because I'm no good." Why? The husband, who speaks approximate French, sets about explaining. When the whites were here there were no tarred roads, no bridges to cross the rivers, no schools for the children and no quinine for malaria. Mwalimwana changed all that. And Saliou has always something bad to say against Mwalimwana. He lacks respect. And now he's out of a job with a wife and three children. This is interesting. If the very people that Saliou claims to defend, reject him, it seems a losing game.

Saliou shrugs his shoulders.

"They're confused."

That's easy to say.

A sort of peace reigns in this village. The second wife has just killed a chicken. They are going to cook a stew in my honor. Everybody's fasting. I'm the only one to eat. Lying in a striped deckchair against the mud wall I feel good. I close my eyes. I return to the darkness of the womb. To the hollow of the maternal womb. Vague images pass through my head like a foetus. The first time I made love. He was somewhat intimidated as well. And afterwards when it was over and things hadn't gone that badly, he was in an even worse state. The next day, it was a Thursday I recall, I was sitting in a rocking chair on our verandah, and there he went on a bicycle, his hair in his eyes, his shirt sticking with sweat to his shoulder blades. He stood up on the pedals and shouted: "I love you!" Fortunately there was nobody around. Only Widow Reynalda watering her bougainvillea on the balcony opposite. A little deaf, she didn't raise an eyelid. I was the victim you might say. Even so, I was rather pleased with this slap at the Mandingo marabout. Later on:

"You're the only woman I've ever loved. In fact, I think I still love you. Do you know whom I married?"

Who? He makes a vague gesture. He lives in Saint Claude, the mulatto paradise. His family might sell the Habitation des Hauteurs Sainte Marie to the local authorities who want to make it into a museum of local history, genuine or not. They'll put in a few stones engraved by the Arawaks or Caribs, a reproduction of the Santa Maria and a portrait of Schoelcher. This is your past, little West Indians. Or they'll make it into a hotel for tired American and Canadian billionaires. He has a villa on the Saintes in an extraordinary setting in the crook of a bay between two rocky sugar loaves. You can only get there by boat. He does a lot of boating, water skiing, scuba diving. Which explains why he is so healthy, despite all the alcohol he takes in. He has two sons.

"Are you going to marry your white man?"

In his eyes it's high treason. I call it sexual patriotism. I don't know where I'm going. I don't know why I'm here. For one moment, I feel good. A small boy, almost naked, stares at me from a distance. I'm a long way away, little man. In my mother's womb which I never should have left.

You'd think it would be easy to make out cards with the following information: Name of father, Name of mother, Profession of mother, Number of children (living, dead), etc., etc. It's an apparently simple job. Well, it isn't. First of all because my ladies don't speak French and I don't speak a word of their language. Secondly, because they have great trouble calculating the age of their children and how many have died. And then they mix up their co-wives' children with their own. In short, it's hopeless. I regularly tear up four yellow cards before getting it right. The worst of it all is that they laugh at me. Kindly, of course. I seem to amuse them a lot. I'm their black Persian. Yehogul tells me again:

"Learn the languages. It's not difficult."

He has achieved a miracle. A foreigner like me, he speaks the country's five main languages. Let's be honest, I'm fed up with the job. But I plod on. The last woman leaves. Her baby is better. His skin is less matt, he's starting to sit up and take interest in his surroundings. He just made it.

"Can I take you home?"

All these men specialize in broken-down cars. We drive off to the sound of old iron.

"Did Saliou tell you?"

What?

"He didn't tell you anything? I see."

What is he talking about? He looks mysterious. He can keep his mysteries. The peace of Diamfamani didn't last very long. I'm living on the edge of exasperation. I'm on a dangerous path, I know: I project my personal frustration onto the country and its people. The call of the muezzin, the sheep droppings, the beggars chanting and even the children's smiles irritate me. Why do they smile? When I don't have the heart to laugh. Yehogul gets me home nevertheless. Abdourahamane comes out, eyes down.

"Someone came. A soldier. He says he'll be right back."

Get him to come back. Get him to come back quickly. To take me away. Away from this town. And approach my island. I'm at the prow of my ship. The waves are breaking over the deck.

The old watchman opens the gates. Agossou greets me. So does Abdoulaye. The master is waiting. Something snaps inside me. I come over all weak. What's going on? He has a severe look.

"Are you enjoying your new duties?"

What is he talking about? Once again, it's obvious the meeting is not going to go the way I'd like it to.

I pull myself together. Ask the question. Is that it? I explain.

"To occupy your time."

"I would have thought you could have found other occupations.

Well, Saliou was right. Ibrahima Sory is a feudal reactionary. At a time when my sisters are preaching women's revolution, he blames me for occupying my time usefully in a dispensary! What would he like me to do? So-called feminine work, like sewing, embroidery and crochet?

"I've already told you, Veronica, I won't do anything to save you."

Save me from what? Am I in danger?

"You should know who Yehogul is. He was driven out of his country for subversive activity. He asked us for political asylum and, despite our opposition, Mwalimwana accepted. Ever since, he has meddled with domestic politics. He has taken sides with the worst kind of fanatic."

I'm telling you I'm fated. I touch a rose and it turns into a cactus. My fingers bleed. All I see in Yehogul is a competent little doctor, interested in his work and slightly paternalistic towards me. I don't have the key to the characters. I take the Jack of Spades for the Jack of Hearts, the King of Clubs for the King of Diamonds . . . It all falls into place now—that's why he's friends with Saliou. I give you my word, I didn't know anything about all that. He's not satisfied. His eyes are penetrating even further.

"What is there between you and Saliou?"

A cop. I realize I'm dealing with a cop. I'm looking for salvation in the arms of a cop.

"In that case, why did you accompany him home?"

Oh no. The interrogation has lasted long enough. If this is all it is, why didn't he call me into his office at the ministry, one cop behind a typewriter, two others guarding the door?

He then says this extraordinary thing:

"You will not leave this house until tomorrow."

But nothing could suit me better. I'd simply like the invitation to be in another tone. Not an order. He becomes polite again.

"Excuse me a moment. Abdoulaye will look after you."

I know the scenario. He'll disappear for hours. I'll thumb through magazines, read, drink grapefruit juice. If I had a bit of respect for myself, I'd leave. But there's a secret unhealthy voluptuousness in being treated like an object. I sink into a sofa covered with animal skins. At least the furniture at Heremakhonon doesn't make me feel sick. If you had to define it, you would say it's rather oriental in style. What a surprise! Ibrahima Sory reappears after a few minutes and sits down beside me.

"I'd like to understand who you are."

Who am I? We have said it over and over again. I'm a down-and-out traveller looking for her identity. Hooligans have stripped me of my papers. I'm lying in a stream, my dress pulled up over my belly. I lie groaning. A couple of whites pass by.

"Can't they go and die in their own country?"

Kiss me, my nigger with ancestors. Let's leave them to fight outside because their mother died when they were twelve. That's not our business. Our mothers will die of old age.

There are times when one outdoes oneself. You don't know why. Times you know you'll remember when you're an old woman, dried out by menopause. Times that make life acceptable, for once you're dead, you can't make love anymore. There are times like that. Afterwards you look at each other. And you know something has changed. Even if you don't admit it. He moves slightly away. I instinctively retain him. He kisses me with unusual gentleness and murmurs:

"Let me go. I have to work."

I'm not starry-eyed. But this familiarity seems revealing. I let him go. Almost happy.

And I remain alone. It's dark in the room. You'd think it's night. Black, curly-haired night, like the *Bête à Man Hibé*. A silver harmonica playing night. That no longer frightens children. Mabo Julie is dead.

But I don't need her hand to get to sleep. Let them talk. I don't care.

"Veronica prefers a servant to her mother."

All the time she was alive, I never knew I loved her. I took her for granted like my right hand or eye. It seemed natural for her to be there to rub me with bay rum when I was hot, to make me drink herb tea or plait my hair with a mixture of palma christi oil and wine.

And that's my worst regret. Never having said:

"Mabo Julie, I love you."

The night is all-embracing. My rabs have left me and gone to Sangomar Point. Yes, I know it's a lure. It's only the senses at peace. Tomorrow they'll be hammering again on the window with their beaks. But tomorrow will never come. The night will set in like *Ado-Kpon.* Men, women and children will change faces. They'll all be nyctalopes. With long, greasy hair like Indians.

The night is perfumed with frangipani. A little like the smell of death. You find it in the cemeteries. Ti-Sapoti is sitting on a grave. He's looking for his father and mother. Watch out, whoever takes him in his arms. But it's not night. It's daytime. The heat has come to a standstill. Time in this country has a slow quality that I have not encountered anywhere in the world. Usually time flies. You've hardly opened your eyes and it's dark again. We are haunted by what we haven't done and what we'd like to do. Nothing like that here. Well, as far as I'm concerned. I suppose things for those who have meetings and are on committees must be different. The main thing is to have something to do then, to create. But what? I can't spend my entire day at the dispensary. Yehogul does. So Yehogul too is a "revolutionary," a "subversive element," to quote the *Quotidien Unique.* I didn't know. He never tried to convert me. He often complains of his work conditions. He also talks about the people's wretchedness. That's all!

Abdoulaye pours me some tea in a little Chinese porcelain cup. I've still got the memory of the previous hours though. Happy? Obviously not. A part of me knows full well that this man won't give me anything. Pleasure. Yes, a lot. Another part delights in passiveness. The sum of the two doesn't make happiness. Surely not. I have been imagining things. I imagined that the afternoon's intimacy meant something. So I wait for Ibrahima Sory with childish anticipation. As if as soon as he gets back he'll suddenly throw off the mask and reveal more than his body. Disappointments of disappointments. The afternoon drags on and changes into night. No Ibrahima Sory. Oh, I can imagine—affairs of state. *L'état, c'est moi* and nothing else. The state should be *my* fantasy and *my* desire. The embroidered pillow case has left a mark on my right cheek. I'm not going to cry, however. Like a silly goose. Let's be cynical—didn't I have my fill this afternoon? No. Do you mean I'm insatiable? I mean my heart's bigger than my sexual appetite. If it wasn't for Yehogul and the ladies at the dispensary I would stay here this morning on the terrace. Waiting. He's bound to come back. Yet I realize it would be pathetic. I still have some pride.

The young soldier is polishing the Mercedes near the garage. I've underrated the courtesy of this man. He doesn't come home at night, but sends me his car. I'd have preferred a message, an explanation. Nothing of the sort. The young chauffeur opens the door for me and clicks to attention. Really. Did I come to Africa for that? Will I find my identity in this role? To hell! Let's forget about my identity. Isn't all this searching in vain? In vain.

At the entrance to the town a long line of cars has come to a standstill and soldiers, their guns slung over their shoulders, are checking papers. They naturally let us through. They even give us a salute. More soldiers in front of the market. In front of the radio station. People are scarce and silent. The blind have forsaken the vicinity of the Matanko mosque. Despite my state of apathy I'm intrigued. What's going on? The chauffeur replies:

"Because of yesterday."

Yesterday? He nods. These people are incapable of giving a coherent, concise explanation. What does he mean? He just repeats:

"Because of yesterday."

Yehogul is not at the dispensary. A few women are sitting on the verandah holding their little yellow booklets. A waste of time asking them. They won't understand. I manage to unearth two nurses in the first aid room. They stare at me in amazement. Don't I know? No, they'll have to explain. I live in another world. A world of soap bubbles.

One of them tells me there was a demonstration yesterday. A

demonstration? Why? Because of this student? Which student? The student they killed. It's not sure, it's not sure they killed him. Oh no? That's what they say. Go on! A demonstration from the Matanko mosque to the Place of the Martyrs. Were there a lot of people? She wasn't there, but her husband was. Mwalimwana didn't like the demonstration, so the soldiers fired. Any dead? Or wounded? They say there were. A lot? A lot? They don't know.

That explains everything. The pieces of the jigsaw are fitting together. I understand why Ibrahima Sory was so intent on interrogating me. Why he stopped me from leaving Heremakhonon. He wanted to protect me in his fashion. Protect me, but what about the others?

The Mercedes is off again. At the Esso garage a taxi driver is patching up an inner tube. We cross the town diagonally. When we draw up level with the soldiers, the chauffeur waves his tricolor party card.

Oumou Hawa is in her compound with her baby on her back. She dips a big wooden spoon into a pot of sauce. That's what courage must be. Letting the daily ritual of life go on unchanged. You'll have to leave me out of this. I haven't got the self-control. She lays down her spoon and points to a stool.

"Saliou will be back for lunch soon."

Oumou Hawa, tell me about yesterday. While I was experimenting with pleasure, others were walking bare-headed under the sun and being sniped at by the cops. They were shedding blood.

"No, there were no deaths. Well, not up till now. A lot of arrests. They say they took them to Samiana . . . "

Samiana! I freeze. The same Samiana?

"There's only one camp at Samiana. It's the worst in the country. They say all kinds of torture are carried out there."

I know how much we can attribute to popular imagination. Some people are always prepared to swear they've seen flying saucers and Martians. Even so, Samiana! He knew how to choose the right spot. Oumou Hawa, where will all this lead to? She holds out her breast to her baby and doesn't answer. I don't know much about these questions—it does seem, however, that if the enemy is all powerful, I mean, if he's the one with the police, the army, the guns and the helicopters, then the struggle doesn't have any meaning. Why then, when you know you're in a losing game?

The baby sucks away with little sighs of contentment.

"Saliou says you've got to fight even so."

Fight with what? Your bare hands? Like the Christians with the lions? Is that what he wants, Saliou: a line of martyrs for the new religion? She changes breasts. Doesn't she have regrets? She could lead a completely different life. Live like her sister, Ramatoulaye, surrounded by Directoire furniture. Or simply live in the north with a pious Moslem who would lay his beads down only long enough to get her with child. Or else . . . she makes a face:

"Regrets? What's the use of regrets?"

I won't get any more out of her, I know. O for the Westernized with their long, psychological explanations, their childhood through a toothcomb and their hairsplitting. I've been told there's no room for personal problems here.

"Let's go inside. It's too hot in the compound."

A noise of backfiring, a screech of brakes and Saliou is back. For the first time since I've known them, each going his own way as if in two separate worlds, I watch Saliou take Oumou Hawa in his arms, squeeze her very tightly and say something softly in her ear. She smiles and I can see that her eyes are full of tears. This woman is suffering. More than I can imagine. But extreme modesty stops her from saying it out loud. As I said, O for the Westernized, the outbursts at first sight, the exhibitionism, the tears, the whole arsenal of pathos. Her headtie has slipped onto her shoulders. Saliou strokes her soft hair plaited in lozenges. She's suffering and didn't tell me.

"Every time I leave home, she's afraid I won't come back alive."

He teases her. As if ashamed of her weakness in my presence, she leaves the room . . . Saliou, why didn't you tell me?

"You've said it often enough. Our problems aren't yours. Yours? Yours? What are yours? Tell me about them. I know nothing about them."

Obviously, mine are ridiculous. Besides they are all confused in my mind for the time being. Tell me about the demonstration.

"They'll tell you there were only a few students and a few hot-headed intellectuals. That's the set phrase. It's not true. The taxi-drivers left their taxis. The market sellers their stalls, the civil servants their offices. Everybody was in the streets."

As I wasn't there, I shall never know the truth. And then if I had been there the prisms of my desires and dreams would have distorted the reality. It's a fact there's no such thing as reality. The facts are made of Venetian glass.

"The only well-organized sectors in this country are . . . the police . . . and the army. It was obvious they had advance knowledge of our project and left nothing to chance."

We're coming to Ibrahima Sory's responsibility. Why his? Doesn't he merely take orders from Mwalimwana? Saliou laughs bitterly.

"Mwalimwana is weak, fairly generous, fairly idealistic. This was evident in the early days of independence. But he had to back down owing to the outcry from the feudal lords in the north who found him too revolutionary. And now two men actually govern this country, Ibrahima Sory and his cousin, Siradiou, Ramatoulaye's husband."

But what do Ibrahima Sory and those of his party, if it is a party, want? It's not out of sadism or senseless cruelty they have men and women shot.

"They belong to another world. They were brought up with a certain idea of Africa. For them, men without a name are scum, good for working in jobs they decide to give them. Oh, they encourage the arts! Have you heard the army's traditional music ensemble? Have you seen the national ballet? They took Paris and New York by storm. The African soul had never been expressed so well. The soul, the soul, they'll kill us to the last man to safeguard it. Whereas we claim it's the body that has to be cured."

This is beyond me. Perhaps if they drew two camps, one imperialist, the other socialist, one pro-Washington, the other pro-Moscow, despite my hatred of slogans, I could work it out. But these subtleties! Because in fact these men are fighting and killing each other in the name of Africa. Because they each love it in their own way, see it in their own way and dream up priorities. Or am I once again over my head? Or are all these words, *soul, body,* but the mask for other realities? I'd need an objective teacher who wouldn't laugh at my ignorance. Does one exist? Everyone takes sides. The unbiased are the down-and-outs like myself, tossed about from one side to another, never knowing what's going on.

"You'd better not come here for a while. We're going to be watched."

What do I risk? Oumou Hawa has laid the table for two as usual. She goes back to her children in the compound. This apparent submission, this apparent detachment hide a world I shall never comprehend. She could be my guide nevertheless. Be the chief linguist who interprets the words of the oracle. Does the road to revolution pass through a man's arms? Does loving a man lead to loving a cause? All you need is to make the right choice. Right, what does that mean?

"You know what I dreamed? Not last night. There was no time to dream last night. That I was a fat, old polygamist. You were sleeping in the room to the right. Oumou Hawa in the room to the left. Revealing, isn't it?"

He wants me to smile. Is it really the time to smile? Then suddenly his expression changes.

"I get very worried about you."

In a way, he's a scream. He gets worried about me. When he admits himself that his house is being watched and his wife cries whenever he goes off. About me. Perhaps he knows that in actual fact I'm the most vulnerable. Now, now, let's not be soft. I've always hated being soft to the point that I wished those ancestors whose pitiful condition they hammered into me had suffered more. To punish them. For what?

For having been conned. The victims are always to blame.

This is no afternoon for wandering around the streets. The soldiers watch me go by without a word however. Illogical. I'd like them to shout at me, assault me, rape me. That would be a way of forcing me to take sides. For some unknown reason, I end up in front of the Hotel de Picardie. Jean Lefevre and Adama greet me with some advice:

"With those trigger-happy bastards, a bullet quickly goes astray. You shouldn't be outdoors."

I sit down between them. What do they think of the demonstration? What do they think? Yes, what do they think?

"They'll kill off the trade. Who'd think of going out for a drink with all that fuzz in the streets?"

These are the unbiased. Who see situations objectively. I don't know why I go on. Do they think they really killed the student? Killed him? Adama is categorical.

"Of course they did! Did you ever see the likes of such savages! It's the white man's lash, that's what they need!"

Jean Lefevre is more subtle.

"Perhaps they didn't kill him. Perhaps they're experimenting on him. They say their camps are worse than the Nazis'."

Here come the flying saucers again. And the zombies leaving their bodies in bed while their spouses coat them with pepper. I haven't the heart to laugh unfortunately. What have I come to look for here?

A glass of pastis? If that's it, then I'm served. If they could see me, wouldn't they be right to laugh? Was it for this that I made those two escapes, those seven hours in a DC-10, that farewell at Le Bourget airport? What's Jean-Michel doing at this moment?

An old decrepit white man pops up in front of me.

"I've seen you before."

Where? In that village near Samiana. He's the owner of the garage *cum* bar. I remember.

"What a mess! What a mess they've made of this country! When we were there, it was the pearl of Africa."

Is this why I travelled 4,000 miles? To drink with a trio of poor bastards. Not that I despise them, mind you.

"They shouted at the top of their voices for independence. Well, now they've got it."

Famous last words.

Go back home, my dear. That's where you need to go to look yourself in the eyes. In the eyes of those you supposedly hate. And those to whom you are a stranger. They told me often enough—that sort are only good for copulating and dancing. Was that true? I never asked myself.

We're four. Just what you need for a game of bridge. I obviously play dummy. This pastis tastes like the Marie Brizard when I was young. Mabo Julie used to say:

"Dip your little finger! Your little finger!"

I preferred dipping my thumb because it was bigger.

What should I do? Go home? The worst is when Ado-Kpon arrives. The bats fly away shrieking. A kind of frenzy grips the town. Which doesn't hide the futility. Futile tom-tom. I didn't say that.

"Four kings, can anyone go better?"

I have a hand of bad luck. *La déveine cé on viê nèg.* Ill fortune is an old nigger. I know, I know, I shouldn't dramatize. Aren't I surrounded by friends?

Adama suggests I stay with them. At least I shall be in safety. Two houseboys in baggy trousers are laying the tables in the dining room. One of them drops the spoons. Jean Lefevre shouts a torrent of abuse.

You'd think I imagined the writing on the blackboard. Didn't I dream it up? Perhaps it was my own conscience materializing? The students are so docile and respectful. It is in their own interest though. With soldiers on duty at the main gate to the Institute. With militia pacing up and down in the yard and daily civic instruction classes by the new director. Now there is a man with ideas. He understands that the apparently disastrous effect of intensive reading of the *Principles of . . .* and the little red book has to be counterbalanced by reading works by nationals. Hence the *Ideals and Thoughts of Mwalimwana* and the like. I have never even thumbed through it. It's in their interest to be docile and respectful. At least in appearance. What goes on behind those looks, under those shaved heads, is not my business. I take my classes, that's what I'm paid for. And handsomely. My monthly salary is four times the average annual income. What a dismal farce, teaching philosophy. Just teaching is a joke. A military supervisor pushes open the door and barks: "Everybody in Amphitheater C."

What do they want them for again? They leave the room clicking their heels. They have been made to march in military style.

The town has resumed its daily routines. The market stinks as usual. There is a long line of jobless in front of the employment exchange. People with nothing to do in front of the radio station. Beggars around the mosques. You might think that nothing has happened. Women wait in front of the dispensary. They remove their toothpicks to greet me. I must love them more than I could ever say. Do I really? Do I love them? In fact, I'm constantly swinging between love and hatred. What I liked the previous day exasperates me the next. Yehogul looks worried. He checks to make sure the door is shut. He likes to play at plotting.

"They interrogated me four times at the main police station."

Interrogated about what? A woman enters. Her magnificent baby is covered with gree-grees. The Mandingo marabout dreamed of having his daughter become a doctor. Perhaps he would be pleased to see me here, even though I'm only filling out cards. Anyway, Saliou had a great idea. These few hours at the dispensary give me a small feeling of being useful. Oh, very small! Yehogul, moreover, constantly repeats that his work is just a drop in the ocean. He's like Saliou— quoting depressing facts and statistics. As if he wanted us never to be in peace. As long as I'm at the dispensary, however, I'm in peace. At long last! Perhaps it's the wrong word: rather a soul at ease.

"I think it's nearly the end for me."

The end? He breaks off. Another woman comes in. Her baby has a matt skin, a swollen belly and yellowish eyes. Yehogul removes the necklace of gree-grees. The mother is too worried to protest. What does he mean, soon up? You might think nothing has happened. Nothing, especially last night when I imagined we had gone beyond the bounds of pleasure. Besides, what does that mean, going beyond the bounds of pleasure? Attain a zone of unreality where soul speaks to soul? The Westernized such as us dream too much. Ibrahima Sory only wants from me what he can take and wants it well done. The baby gives a feeble, sickly cry. The mother is reassured. He'll recover. It's only a mild diarrhea. Yes, the Mandingo marabout dreamed of having a doctor in the family. As I was the most intelligent of the three, it was up to me. It was a tacit agreement that I harshly broke off. They had that against me too. But why did I have to satisfy their pride?

"I believe they're going to deport me."

Let's get back to earth. Yehogul washes his small, plump hands. Bishop's hands, as they say. Bishop Duchapuis' in any case looked like sugar tongs. I noticed.

"Deport you, why?"

"They have no proof, but they'll make some up. That won't bother them."

What should I say? If he's deported, then naturally I'll be sorry. But is this about me being sorry? As in all other cases, it's not a question of my personal feelings. Yehogul has a wife and six or seven children. What a life if such a man is your father. I can imagine you must have the same aversion to the words—people, revolution and justice—as I did to race, intelligence and distinction, and that you have nothing better to do than to rush to become respectable. Such is the way of the world. My analysis is not at all correct. If it were, I'd be fighting beside Saliou and Yehogul. Or else I haven't been able to take my refusal to its conclusion. My revolt is a lure. This piece of truth hits me and goes to my head. I have never realized it so clearly. In fact I'm not escaping from anything. Through Ibrahima Sory I'm trying to get back to them on an idealized level. Rid of their absurdities. Entitled to be what they were—arrogant and contemptuous. O Lord, we thank you for having made us different—may the famous prayer no longer have an absurd taste for me. To sum up, I'm not trying to escape them. But to justify myself. It's not surprising then that Ibrahima Sory denies me the love which, according to my theory, could save me. He's got better things to do with a half-caste.

I go out onto the terrace. The last women are waiting. The old watchman, who despite his hernia, has just gotten his wife with child, has closed the gates. It's not the first time, but perhaps never as clearly, I realize my place is not here. At least what I came to do is absurd. Yet I know I won't move. Held back by a hope I know is thwarted from the start.

At the Plaza they're playing *The Valley of Black Gold*. No revolution here—the cowboys of my childhood continue to make the crowds just as stupid. Not *my* childhood: I only went to the cinema to see carefully selected films. Still I did see Shirley Temple surrounded by her pickaninnies. I can still hear the little shoe-shine boy rolling the whites of his eyes in his black face and saying:

"Why do they call a boot a boot, Miss Shirley?"

Everybody laughed. I suffered, I was sick. Literally.

"Didn't you like the film? What a difficult child!"

Next to the Plaza there's a bar for prostitutes. To my surprise there are a lot of prostitutes in this town. Very young girls, badly made-up in leather mini-skirts. It pains me to look at them. No it doesn't. They bother me. Poverty and destitution don't. There have always been rich and poor everywhere. But prostitution! It's all very well saying that it's the oldest profession in the world. But on a closer look you see that it's just another invention that Africa didn't make. Add writing and gunpowder and the list gets longer. These prostitutes bother me. They're proof that Europe has been through these parts. I find myself beyond what they call the dike in the

Carenage district. What was I going to do so far from home? I don't remember. Perhaps just look. The men were wearing torn vests. Ever since then, the contradictory idea of poverty and debauchery are associated in my mind with this masculine piece of underwear and I am grateful to the underwear manufacturers influenced by the USA for dressing men in T-shirts. I'm sure I could never make love to a man in a vest.

The women were badly made-up, broad-beamed as well. Oh, broad-beamed. I learned later that this particular conformation is called steatopygia. Back home I looked at my flat buttocks in the mirror and felt a great relief. As for my mother, though, the sight of her buttocks would shock me and drive me to despair. I got the impression that the God they were thanking daily must have secretly enjoyed himself. These buttocks were the original stygma! The women wore vulgar, flowery dresses and high-heel shoes. Their hair, straightened out with dollops of vaseline, frizzed round their heads. It gave me a shock when I saw Aunt Paula for the first time, lording it in her Hotel Le Relais des Isles. I had to overcome my nausea because I needed her. I was all confusion and chaos. So this retired prostitute, who still bore the traces, was my father's sister. They had been carried in the same womb, locked in its opaque and beneficial darkness. Aunt Paula stroked my cheek:

"So he's your little sweetheart! Well, well, well!"

Yes, these prostitutes bother me. Yet they fascinate me and I enter the bar. The one sitting on my left is barely sixteen. She's drinking a glass of beer. She has a rough voice and red eyes.

"Where're you from, sister?"

Sister? I know it doesn't mean a thing; it's a form of politeness. Alas! I have the unfortunate habit of seeing symbols everywhere. I explain. It is obvious she has no idea of geography and I could just as well be from Mars. She doesn't hide her surprise.

"And there are Blacks in those countries too?"

Oh dear, oh dear. Wasn't it you who sold us? Well, not her. The only thing this poor child ever sold must have been her arse. And cheap, I imagine. Given the general standard of living.

"Are you paying for a drink?"

If I asked her straight off: "What brought you here to this bar stool, this tiny skirt that hardly covers your legs which, as a Moslem, you should be hiding?" What would she reply? I can guess. She wouldn't be offended. She would tell me straight like the young soldier at Samiana: "There's a lot of unemployment around."

The waiter pours her a beer. Me, a second grapefruit juice. I draw up closer. She has a strangely familiar smell of perfume, cheap powder and sweat. Lisette smelled like that. A little servant who used to come and pick us up from school when Mabo Julie was unable to make it.

What does she think of Mwalimwana's regime and the recent demonstration?

"Do you write for the newspaper?"

No, I'm not a journalist, you needn't worry about that. I'm a sister who's up the creek and would like to understand. She looks around, then spits violently on the ground. (This says a lot with very little.) Two men enter the bar. She is no longer interested in me. I'm back in the wet heat of the street. Not far from the bar is the market. And in front of the market, Ramatoulaye's chauffeur, his arms laden with embroidered clothes. Ramatoulaye is in the Mercedes, visibly displeased since I never come to see her. If I told her it is because of her furniture, she'd think me mad. Because she's proud of her Directoire furnishings, just as the Mandingo marabout had been.

"There's something rather strange about your father."

Who'd dare say that? It could only be Jean-Marie, of course. He persisted.

"Do you love your father?"

I said yes, as I didn't dare bring my hatred out in the open. What about him, didn't he love his father?

"The bastard, I hope he kicks the bucket."

The unfortunate father was undergoing a highly delicate operation at that precise moment in a luxury clinic. He survived— thank goodness no child's wish has ever killed his parents. And his mother, did he love his mother? He hesitated.

"Poor soul."

My lovers have always ridiculed my family. In a way, I chose them so that they could do it for me. Jean-Michel was howling:

"Your sisters, your sisters, what a picture! And their husbands!"

What would he say if I put him face to face with Ibrahima Sory? He wouldn't laugh, that's for sure.

Ramatoulaye has changed perfumes and replaced her Carita wig with a head-tie almost six feet long. Would I come with her to Oumou Hawa's? Her baby is ill.

"Oumou Hawa is killing our mother and the old man as well. She has always been his favorite."

What a horrible habit, preferring one child to another. Love should be given equally to all. This is how it would be, I think, if I were a mother. But, of course, I shall never give birth. Do I feel like seeing Oumou Hawa and Saliou? No, I feel like drifting across town, bumping into beggars, whores and soldiers. Sheep escaped from a neighboring compound bar the road. The Mercedes is blocked. Ramatoulaye puts her head out of the window and out of her mouth comes a cataract of words whose meaning I can only guess since I haven't made any progress in learning the national languages. The Mercedes finally forces its way through and speeds off. A young boy launches a gob of spit in its direction with all his might. That's the second in one day. Our eyes meet. He outstares me. As in those children's games where you try to see who blinks first. He has Birame III's intelligent, sensitive face. Perhaps it's Birame III appearing right in the middle of the market's garbage to remind me? No, the sun is too hot on my head. He comes closer.

"You called me?"

Did I call him? Now that he's a few steps away, I can't retreat. And after all, this spitting has to be explained.

He laughs. A defiant laugh.

"Are you from the police?"

Now, do I look as though I'm from the police? I've been insulted quite a bit up till now, but not to that extent. I'm a foreigner. Pitchforked here.

"Black American?"

These damned black Americans have captured the limelight because of Mahalia, Aretha and James Brown. All we can offer is the cooing of Gilles Sala who is obviously no match. He walks beside me, his thin naked feet in plastic sandals all torn to shreds. He's on his guard and hostile. If I said:

"Please help me." He'd laugh at me and take me for another idiot. This country's overflowing with idiots, I mean foreign idiots. The most common species is the one that exclaims at the slightest object, the slightest gesture:

"They're divine!"

And considers Africa the rejuvenation of his Western soul, exhausted and dried up by the technological age. They have more or less given up washing and learned the local languages. Are they sincere? Do they really believe that Africa has nothing else to do but give and give? Men to dig and shovel with the whip behind them; spices, gold and ivory for ladies' necklaces; now balms and ointments . . . But is it up to me to criticize? When I too have my hand outstretched. I'm a first rate beggar. A parasite. A louse.

Now what do I do?

I wake up the chauffeur who is asleep with a handkerchief tied around his forehead. He stares at me in terror. From what abyss have I drawn him? Come on, get your engine started. Heremakhonon is always open to me. Whether the master is there or not, that's what they told me. Let's admit it, I've made one step forward. I've been promoted to the rank of object whose constant presence makes for the pleasantness of the place. I'm an arum in a vase. I say arum because the plant is exotic like me. It doesn't grow here.

Three

There are times when you feel like letting yourself go. You can't go round in circles at the Institute week in and week out. From my villa to the Institute. From the Institute to Heremakhonon. With short detours to the dispensary, to Saliou's or the Hotel de Picardie. Like an old couple walking round the Place de la Victoire. From the bandstand to the central alley; from the alley to the sea front. And back. For the moment I can't go on.

It's true I have a stay-at-home nature. I abhor physical exercise (except for making love, of course). I've always believed that sport should be left to the dunces. And they taught me that dancing and auxiliary pleasures are outlets for those who can lay claim to nothing else. Despite these convictions, I'm suffocating. The end of the day is humid and torrid as I rightly or wrongly imagine the south of the United States to be. Soon the unending night will have to be rowed through. It's almost adolescent—pent-up desires and nobody to satisfy them. In these countries where the telephone is a luxury, the quickest way of communicating is to send your houseboy with a scribbled note. I could notify Adama who would slip on her silk dress to escort me wherever I wanted. But I shudder at the sight we would make. Two whores out hunting. That leaves Pierre-Gilles, the bachelor expatriate who comes across the street to chat and have a drink. I know he's a homosexual and in love with a young Fula whom he has employed and is trying to keep prisoner like Albertine. Unfortunately, the young Fula is heterosexual and accepts his desires for the same sad reason: "Unemployment, sister, unemployment."

He is having an affair with Mariama, a pretty young girl who looks after the children three villas up the road. You may wonder why out of so many expatriates, healthy in mind and body, I have chosen this one. The reason is obvious. Their good health frightens me; they have their hands full with children, farmhouses to do up in Normandy, watermills in Dordogne, boats and bank accounts. They have clearcut opinions on things and people. Pierre-Gilles is the only one with whom I have any similarities.

My sudden invitation undoubtedly surprises him and he's not very keen. The young Fula is arranging records with one knee on the floor. He has the unbending slenderness of Ibrahima Sory. His hands are extraordinarily slim.

"Where do you want to go exactly?"

Where? There must be a place in town where you can have a good time. Where you can let yourself go. Where you can remember you're young and where death's drum cannot be heard. The young Fula murmurs:

"Miami Club."

Pierre-Gilles immediately flies into a temper. When did he go there? And with whom? Oh, why don't they keep their scenes until later. Pierre-Gilles is good-looking. He must have had quite a number of proposals in Paris. Alas, he seems to have an exotic taste. He confided in me that he had been in love with a third secretary at the Japanese embassy and wanted to take his life when the latter was transferred to Malaysia. Instead of committing suicide, however, he left for Africa and here he is caught up with an impossible love. For want of a better word!

He's not too keen on accompanying me. Because he knows that once he has turned his back, the young Fula will be off to see Mariama. And yet he's a friend who has guessed that things are not going too well. He gives in then.

"In any case, it's too early to go out."

So it is! So let's drink in preparation for this mad night of deliverance. He looks at me openly worried by my exuberance.

"Has your minister ditched you?"

He's the only one I confide in more or less. Ditched? No. There are merely times when I cannot bear the unchanging and frustrating schema of my relations with him. It's as if a temperamental film director, rehearsing the same sequence, arrived at the same place each time and shouted: "Cut!"

I have even realized that it's only my impatience or dreams that vary the pleasure of our meetings. For him it's always the same. I mean it's pleasure, period. So let's drink! Another reason why I like the company of Pierre-Gilles. Because he has tried to give what they call a soul, for want of a better word, to his house. Most expatriates live in dull administration housing where the furniture is the same, floor after floor. Saliou and Yehogul live with a bare minimum. Pierre-

Gilles drives miles to buy a mask, a blanket or an object. He pursues his search with the same energy as he does love. Jobaliped is written on a tapestry he's just brought back from the North. So he's been to the North! He shrugs his shoulders.

"Poorer, even more wretched than the rest of the country. Another world, fanatical and medieval."

Oh, don't spoil my picture. My picture of a region where I shall never go. Actually, if they invited me to go to the North, I would refuse. I realize the danger of such an undertaking. Alfa serves a whiskey. He doesn't drink himself. A Moslem never drinks alcohol, he reminds me. Obviously I could snigger and recall in turn that the Koran also prohibits sodomy. But that would be too easy. Alfa's a victim. Pierre-Gilles too. And what about me? All in all we're three victims in this living room. Why not each confess and compare our experiences? Pierre-Gilles is attracted to the idea. Alfa looks at us with surprise. Say what? About whom? Everything. Father. Mother. Brothers and sisters. The first woman he had. He loved. He laughs. He obviously thinks we're cracked. Besides he says so.

"The whites are crazy."

To be more exact he should have said the whites and their disciples. Or the whites and their creatures. But this abridged version that includes me merely adds punch. I don't particularly like the way the night is beginning. With these killjoy statements. If Alfa discloses not what we want him to disclose but what is dear to him there is no doubt that his tale would be something else. A long struggle to learn the rudiments of writing, to feed himself, to clothe himself, to exist.

I'm ashamed.

"My mother is a very talented pianist. She plays Debussy."

(Obviously it's Pierre-Gilles speaking). Not like my mother who bravely tapped away with her Chopin.

"My brother's also very good. He has earned his reputation as a concert pianist."

I know. The scenario is so familiar. The unloved son who doesn't play the game they expect him to play. We are starting out the night very badly. Really very badly.

"The person I loved the most? Apart from my mother, of course, who'll never know . . . "

Pierre-Gilles, Pierre-Gilles, we're starting badly. Let's escape. Let's drink. After the third whiskey everything gets better. Not that we see everything through rose-colored glasses. But we start to float, leaving behind the cohort of our fantasies.

Pierre-Gilles has a dark blue Fiat that starts in a tenth of a second. He pretends not to notice Alfa hurriedly closing the garage doors.

The Miami Club is at the exit to the town at the end of a long gravel drive. At first we can only make out a square building looming in the night with a number of people idly standing about. One of them hurries to open the bright red door for us, hoping for a few francs . . . which Pierre-Gilles liberally gives him. Like me, he keeps his conscience clear as best he can. We enter a hallway. A young boy seated behind a table hands us our tickets without a look. We push aside a scarlet velvet curtain just as filthy as the rest and the dance floor emerges. Full to bursting point. To the left a small platform on which a band is playing. To the right, a small bar besieged by customers. Seeing us as important guests the manager rushes up and seats us as best he can. Looks are friendly, which surprises me. In fact, the people here are too hospitable. I imagine the effect that Pierre-Gilles and myself would have in some village hall in the West Indies. Or at the Caribbean festival in Paris. The black berets. Nothing like that here. The very young, the young and the not so young dancing away their cares to Africanized versions of Rhythm n' Blues, drinking and laughing at the top of their voices. Who are they? What are they doing? Who are their heroes? What are their dreams? Their desires? They are somewhere between the masses lining up at the water tap or the dispensaries, for whom French is a totally foreign language and whose world is limited to the frontiers of the country, and the minority who lays down the laws or contests them. They are already privileged. They have already solved their basic problems. They already have leisure time. A woman, or rather a young girl, comes up to us, smiling and trying to wiggle her hips, although her heavy heeled shoes are a handicap.

"I see you're with us tonight sister."

There is a moment's hesitation. Then I recognize her, the little prostitute from the Alcatraz bar. She asks in a familiar tone:

"Is he your husband?"

Husband, like sister, doesn't mean anything. It's a polite expression to denote the person you go to bed with. To give weight to my affirmation Pierre-Gilles feels bound to kiss me tenderly. He smells of Arden for Men, an after-shave that I once liked very much . . . No, stop the memories. Let's live this night in the present. Her name is Kadidiatou, which delights Pierre-Gilles. She declines a drink and goes off promising to come back soon. The most logical thing to do in a dance hall when you are two, or appearing to be a couple, is to dance. And that's what we do. Pierre-Gilles, I must confess, is a much better actor than I am. He holds me tight in his arms, cheek to cheek. For the onlooker, the illusion must be perfect.

Wish I was back
In your arms,
In your arms,
Oh what could I do
What could I do.

The singer's accent is by no means perfect. You might think him absurd in his jeans that are too tight, his studded jacket and imitation Afro. But nobody seems to mind. A red light, supposed to be more intimate, has cast its glow. I stay too lucid, too intrigued by these men and women with whom I have not come into contact until now. They too are Africa. But an Africa already painted with a Western varnish. They have cast off the boubou. Obviously you don't dance in a boubou. It hinders your movements. The hoped-for liberation has not yet been reached. How many more whiskies will I need? There was a time when I didn't need any to grow wings. To fly effortlessly to the top of the ylang-ylang tree whose white blossom, when kept in alcohol, gives off a peppery perfume. Sitting on a cloud I surveyed the island covered with lilies and bougainvillea. After all I could have answered:

"You too are the only man I ever loved."

There, I am being sentimental again. It would have been a cliché. It's common knowledge we're always looking for the same man, lover after lover.

"You don't look as though you're enjoying yourself very much."

To be truthful, I'm not. I'm afraid the evening isn't very

successful after all. A waiter brings us a bottle of champagne wrapped in a none too clean rag in an ice bucket and points to a kind of mastodon, the type of man I can't stand, with his head as polished as a mirror and bright, staring eyes, dressed in a brown gandourah and patent leather shoes.

"This is from Baké for Mademoiselle."

Who is Baké? He looks surprised. I don't know Baké? Baké is a big businessman who owns the only non-nationalized shops in the country. Even Mwalimwana is afraid of him. Pierre-Gilles is delighted. He nods and smiles to the Baké in question to thank him. Let's open the bottle then. I don't quite know how but we've got into conversation with a couple sitting at the next table. They join us. The circle gets bigger. Four glasses are poured out. We laugh. Don't ask me about what. We talk. I don't know about what either. I think it's me who's talking. And laughing. Kadidiatou comes back, asks how I am and whispers:

"Baké likes you very much."

She then smiles at Pierre-Gilles whom she has no intention of offending. He could only be flattered by his wife's success. She sits next to me and whispers:

"You can have everything with Baké."

Everything? Meaning what? She makes a wide gesture.

"Money. Jewels. A car. He's a friend of Mwalimwana. They were children together."

Why isn't he a minister as a token of their long friendship? She laughs.

"He can't read or write."

This is missing from my collection, an illiterate lover!

She goes off, called back by her duties at the bar. The wife then tells me:

"She's a whore."

No contempt. Just like saying he's a businessman. Or he's an invalid. Stating the facts. How do they see each other? The husband asks me to dance. This is too absurd. I'm not enjoying myself. I want to go home.

The light has changed and dyed the men's shirts indigo. Pierre-Gilles, the only white man in the place, looks like a saint in a stained glass window. If I told him I want to go home, he would only be too glad after all. By this time Alfa must be working Mariama up to an orgasm and laughing with her about his master's demands.

"The whites are mad."

I'd laugh too if they hadn't dragged me along with them. And there's no cure for this type of madness. What did I expect, coming here to this dance hall? It's inhabited by familiar faces, each with a different expression. Mockery—contempt—surprise. Saliou is looking at me reproachfully. He must be at his wit's end trying to win me over to their side. To get me away from Ibrahima Sory. Conversions are not made by force. Above all, don't think of Ibrahima Sory. The waiter brings a plate loaded with hot skewered lamb, covered in pimentos.

"It's Baké . . ."

But Baké's disappeared. At the table he was occupying there remain three men and a very pretty woman in a gold lamé boubou, masticating a kola nut and looking absent.

We've all become the greatest of friends. A man and another woman have joined us. Pierre-Gilles puts his hand on my thigh. The good looks of the newcomer to our table have aroused his senses. They bring me too out of my semi-torpor. What does he do? First, what's his name? He is troubled by this dual attention. He stammers.

"Amar. I work for Comarex."

What's Comarex? It sounds like a make of condoms.

"The national shoe company."

He gets bolder. He'll send me some pretty leather slippers.

"Leave him to me."*

We're the only ones who know English at our tables so Pierre-Gilles does not risk being understood. But why should I obey him? It's obvious all the chances are on my side. Homosexuality is a luxury this young boy can certainly not afford. Unless Pierre-Gilles lays it on thick. Which would be indecent in such a place.

There's no doubt I'm chalking up points. Amar asks me to dance. I do my best to chalk up more and the blue light is conducive to my task. Real child's play! They get so worked up these young employees from Comarex.

Pierre-Gilles has had to resign himself to asking one of the women to dance and whispers his spite as he goes by. This

---

*In English in the original.

stranger's mouth has a pleasant taste of ginger and the pulsations of his virile member are wonderfully rhythmic. Nobody except Pierre-Gilles and the unfortunate lady companion stranded at the table pays any attention to us. The light gets bluer and bluer. Even so, my first thought would be to give him an eau de cologne if the adventure is to go any further. Obviously it isn't. Why not? It would make a change from my nigger with ancestors. Out of pure perversity, Pierre-Gilles intervenes on the next dance. Visibly disappointed, Amar goes and sits down, refusing to ask any other partner. He watches us from the table.

"I'm doing this for your good. His wife will end up tearing out your eyes."

Amar has already said that it's not his wife: a girl whom he doesn't like and who clings to him. He's still at the stage where they lie. He's still pure in other words. The arousal from the previous fondling carries over onto Pierre-Gilles. Especially as his Arden for Men rallies a host of souvenirs. And he seems perfectly equipped for giving pleasure. Incurably homosexual? He laughs. I suppose he's flattered.

"Do you want to try?"

Has he already tried?

"Once with a cousin . . . called Sandra. She was half-English."

Mind! We're falling back into the rut. However, I try not to react. I ask questions instead. Did it work?

"More or less! It was later with a woman I loved very much . . . "

Haven't we decided to live tonight in the present? Instead we're drawing circles around ourselves. We're looking for our lost ones. The light comes back just in time to prevent us from sinking further. And standing near our table is gentleman Baké, accompanied by one of his lieutenants. He has exchanged his gandourah for a well-cut European suit, I do declare. He greets me and asks with authority:

"Are you coming to dance, Mademoiselle?"

I shall never know why I refuse. A pure drunken whim? Because I've drunk quite a bit. Is it because he looks like Dr. Carzavel? And consequently the Mandingo marabout and all the clique? Is it because there's too great a distance between Pierre-Gilles' arms and his? Millions of light years. Is it to please Amar who is looking at us?

It goes quiet around us.

Baké repeats more loudly:

"Are you coming to dance?"

This time it's an order. I persist in shaking my head without saying a word. And then Amar gets up in silence. Half drunk too as he has had time to drink profusely, frustrated perhaps at not understanding the game Pierre-Gilles and myself are playing with him, and spurred on I imagine by a childish desire of bravado:

"Mademoiselle says she doesn't want to dance."

Everything happens very quickly. Baké's lieutenant presses on his shoulder and tries to make him sit down, while Baké continues to stare at me as if nothing has happened. Amar refuses to sit down. His companion implores him. He slaps her. She shouts. A man gets up from a nearby table, pushes Amar who hits him. And suddenly a fight breaks out. The band stops. The manager runs up. Glasses roll on the floor. Someone shouts: "Call the police."

I can see blood on Amar's face. I hear shouts. The light goes out. Or does it? And I'm outside in the night as black as can be. My hand in Pierre-Gilles'. People are running. A fleet of cops arrives.

For a successful night, it was really successful! At dawn my innards rendered up the mixture of beer, whiskey and champagne. Now I've got a splitting headache. And in our escape I must have knocked myself as my shoulder is hurting. What a dismal night!

Abdourahamane says that quinqueliba has many virtues in such cases. Done for quinqueliba! Frankly, it's enough to put you off going out at night. Perhaps we dreamed it all? Amar with blood on his face. Baké and his thick lips. This strange, unknown crowd, bent on pleasure. Pierre-Gilles doesn't see things as darkly as I do and tells me I'm dramatizing. He proudly recalls that I tried to rape him, imitates Baké and ascertains that all in all he had a good time. He's lucky. The tenth cup of quinqueliba doesn't manage to wash away the taste of futility and inanity.

Somebody knocks at the door. Abdourahamane announces with his usual ellipsis: "The chauffeur's here."

This is the first time a call from Ibrahima Sory leaves me cold. Shall I stay in bed? My hesitation is brief, I must confess.

Outside the sun lets fly its darts. On closing the door, the chauffeur remarks on my health. I must look awful! Now that we are leaving town I notice for the first time a board marked Comarex. A low wall. A gate painted red. An arrow indicating the parking lot. What do I expect to see? A watchman in khaki comes up. What shall I ask him? If he knows an employee called Amar? And then what? I realize I'm being absurd. We drive on.

At Heremakhonon the sequence starts as usual. The master is waiting for me in his favorite little room. He is dressed somewhat negligently in baggy trousers and a small white silk embroidered boubou, cut in a V at the neck. He makes no comment about my health, says he is pleased to see me and teasingly hands me a tiny gourd containing a brown ointment.

"Would you please massage me? Are women taught to do this where you come from?"

I confess this is not part of our basic education. But I'll try. The ointment has a strong, spicy perfume. Where does it come from? Has a marabout concocted it with a little human blood, hair and nails? He laughs.

"Of course, of course. My mother's just sent it and God knows what it contains."

I massage him as best I can, although if one of us should be treated it should be me. His torso is straight and soft under my hands. He half opens his eyes and I'm struck by their expression of extreme vigilance in contrast to his attitude of abandonment. He closes them again.

"Veronica, I'm a very patient man. There's a wealth of patience in me. But I advise you not to go too far."

The tone is courteous, almost affable. Surprised, I lay down the gourd of ointment on the table. What does he mean? He straightens himself up, lays back against a cushion and looks at me.

"Believe me, I'm sorry I have so little time to spend with you. I understand that sometimes you feel like enjoying yourself. But do you really have to frequent disreputable dance halls, full of drunkards and whores, and get into brawls . . . ?"

When will I keep in mind that I'm dealing with a cop? Useless denying the facts. Let's just point out that his zealous informers have considerably worsened them. He is not listening and is speaking with restrained violence which does not call for an answer.

"Because of you I have been terribly humiliated. Baké came to see me this morning, naturally without knowing there is anything between us. He told me everything."

Now this is getting interesting! That fat pretentious pig complained he had been refused a dance. What was he hoping for? A decree from the Minister for the Interior to force me?

"He didn't complain about you . . . But about the boy who insulted him, who tried to hit him in public and whom the police arrested for drunken behavior."

Insulted! Hit! Whom the police arrested!

"He wanted to make sure that he would receive the punishment he deserves. I couldn't refuse Baké, could I?"

The last words were said with a genuine cruelty. I'm speechless.

Literally, the room starts to turn. Baké is lying. He's lying. And because of his tales, poor Amar . . . What will they do to him? Ibrahima Sory remarks:

"Women's tears have a particularity of always coming after the events."

Does that mean I'm crying? Then it's out of anger. Because Amar did nothing. Nothing.

At the same time, he draws me up against him, unhooks my belt, undoes the buttons on my blouse. I should, I know, protest and break away in horror. Try to get justice for Amar. Easier said than done. He asks mockingly:

"The white man you were with, is he interested in women now?"

I'm too tired. To defend Amar. To defend myself. Defend myself against what? Against desire? I've already lost all willpower.

The wings, which the day before didn't manage to get me off the ground, have spread. I'm rising vertically above the ylang-ylang and from there I can see the bloodwort. Scarlet. Scarlet like human blood. I can see blue sea too like the indigo cloth of the dye workers in Kano. I have never been to Kano. But I know the emir's palace is in gold. Shaku Umar has found his mother again. At Ber Kufa. Somewhere in the villa a bell rings. He moves. Somebody knocks discreetly at the door. It is the first time this has happened while we are together. He sighs.

"It's Abdoulaye . . . I have an important ministerial meeting at five."

What do they do at their incessant meetings and councils?

"Drought . . . We must prevent famine. The army will be brought in."

He picks up his clothes off the floor and gets dressed. For him the intermission is over. It's too bad for me if it's only the intermission that counts. I make a desperate attempt to catch his attention. Perhaps I'm not threatened with famine like the men and women from Begemder. But even so I do deserve some attention. He's already a thousand miles away and quickly strokes my cheek while leaving.

"Go and chat with Ramatoulaye. She's very fond of you."

All these people are very fond of me. Baké, Ramatoulaye . . I could cry.

Agossou is at his post, behind a curtain of giant rose bushes. He gives me a wicked wink. Abdoulaye approaches softly. What would I like to order from the cook for dinner? He's right. We must eat in this world. In actual fact, Abdoulaye is the African male version of Mabo Julie. The same attention and no reward expected. Beings born to serve. But while Mabo sang and chatted in the kitchen, he serves in silence. Silent and hieratic, like his master. I've got a bad conscience now. You might even say I'm suffering. That's how my night ended! My need for an execution has claimed a victim. Perfectly innocent. What will they do to this boy? All they can accuse him of is unruly behavior in public. That can't be very serious. Even if Baké has intervened? I need to confide and be reassured at the same time. Saliou, only Saliou . . .

Abdoulaye joins me near the gate. Without looking up he explains that the Minister will not like it if I go back to town so quickly. Well let the Minister get angry. I put up with his absences. I am very clear-headed now. His presence spoils everything and curbs my resources.

Taxis are scarce in this area. A line of luxury cars in front of the Ghanaian ambassador's residence and two guards in livery. A reception at the well-to-do's. At last a taxi stops in which two Al Hadji masked in white are seated.

Saliou is alone. I didn't know their newly-born had been hospitalized and Oumou Hawa is staying with him, which they now allow at the Jomo Kenyatta hospital. He has had to send the other two children to his eldest brother in Tenigbé. He didn't know what to do with them. Is it to this man hounded by domestic worries that I'm going to tell my absurd misdeeds? No need to tell them, he knows! And I can see that his version is no different from Ibrahima Sory's: Amar is the assailant! Oh no, let's get the facts right . . . He shrugs his shoulders.

"Do you know how many political prisoners there are in this country's camps? How many heads of families are arrested every day for 'breach of opinion'?"

I don't know in fact.

" . . . and you imagine that friends will get worked up about a piece of arse?"

A piece of arse! He's right, but arse or not there's an innocent victim of injustice.

He answers drily: "We're political militants. Not knight errants."

This means that Amar can go and . . . ? I had no intention of making a martyr out of him. I was just interested in his fate.

"Since Baké has intervened personally, they'll stick a fine on him or one or two months in prison. Nothing more."

Nothing more! And that's Saliou talking! With such indifference! You could even say with cruelty. He shakes his head.

"You're incredible. You accept Birame III's death without blinking. And here you are all worked up on account of a little hustler you met in a night club."

That's below the belt. Of course I could defend myself and explain. But why bother? Let them all die! Pile up in their prisons! Disappear from the face of the earth!

"You refuse to understand!"

Oh, I'm sorry, I've understood perfectly. There are some prisoners, some dead who are not worth worrying about. The revolution doesn't even want them for its dung heap.

Why did I ever leave Heremakhonon? A few pricks of conscience for a night club hustler? I must be mad.

Quick, a taxi! And I'll ask Abdoulaye to cook me a dish with a complicated name that looks like calaloo when I was a child. You add annatto leaves, okra, crab and peppers. Especially peppers to chase the spirits and ghosts away. I'm rambling. So what.

We pass in front of the main police station which, mea culpa, I have never looked at so intently. A several storeyed building. In the yard, black marias with a red light on top, as sinister as a bleeding eye. Shall I go in and enquire about Amar? I'd probably make things worse. Better keep quiet. Draw a line. Saliou is the first disappointment.

Abdoulaye greets me with satisfaction. I have learned to read this face that gives nothing away. Stiff, grey eyelids, like the clams I used to wrench from the seabed. The protruding forehead like a calabash. The hollow cheeks. Who teaches them this impassiveness, this self-control? Is the exuberant nigger, spontaneous like a child, another of Europe's inventions? No. They're not niggers. But we are!

We, the so-called Diaspora! They're not niggers, but Africans. For many, unfortunately, the process of negroization seems to have already begun. To hell with these thoughts! Go away! Obey the master. Cross the garden and go chat with Ramatoulaye. I'll just have to forget about her furniture.

Ramatoulaye has just come back from the reception at the Ghanaian embassy where the ambassador's wife was holding her weekly tea party. With a sigh of relief, Ramatoulaye removes her heavy wig which makes her look like one of the Supremes. Her hair emerges, rose-plaited. Now here is someone who niggerfies herself for pleasure! Shall I warn her? That's how it all began. Tegbessu's apparently innocent desire to be carried by porters. Agadja's wish to play the organ. It didn't look like much. And then everything got messy. Europe must be kept at a distance at any price. Surprisingly, Ramatoulaye doesn't think I'm mad. She answers sadly: "We can't. Basically that's the tragedy of this country. People like Ibrahima Sory who try to save the past are called reactionaries, a new word. It is said they want to mystify the people, exploit them, all new words. They say you have to progress. Progress, what's that?"

She brushes her wig in short strokes.

"What is it? My children ridicule everything I believe in."

Oh no, we're not going to sink into melancholy. I am fed up with melancholy. I'm telling you, there is something in this country which, no matter what you try, ends up in regret, remorse and disillusionment. Fortunately, Hafsa brings Ramatoulaye her new baby, the fifth in five years. Ramatoulaye sighs. We talk about birth control. The pill. Coils. These are highly feminine subjects and not demoralizing. The gentleness of the evening at Heremakhonon takes me by surprise each time. Perhaps it's due to the big trees. The flowers. The silence. Especially the silence. A servant in the outhouses is playing an instrument I can't identify. Always the same tune. I can hear laughter from Ibrahima Sory's brothers and nephews who live in a part of the villa I have never penetrated. The tiles of the terrace are hot, like the rocks of the River Rose after absorbing a full day's sun. The washerwomen are up to their calves in water, their dresses rolled up over their black, shiny legs, then knotted at the thigh. The froth from the soap breaks away in streaks. Yes, one can forget everything. One can lean back in time. I want that less and less, I realize. As if the present had caught up with me. Not that I've won anything in exchange. I even prefer my old ghosts. They were good company: they didn't have blood on their faces. Well, his evening at the Miami Club and two dances with a stranger will have cost him dearly. He must be cursing us now. Not that his curse will have much effect. They won't stop Pierre-Gilles from screwing Alfa. As for me . . . Such is life!

The gates of the garden open and then close again. The noise of a car engine. The Minister is back. I hear his footsteps. He comes and sits next to me. With a gesture whose humility cuts me each time, Abdoulaye changes his babouches and retires.

"I spent the entire ministerial meeting thinking of you."

This is an enormous confession: I ought to be flattered.

"I was wondering whether Abdoulaye would manage to retain you. Or whether tomorrow morning I wouldn't hear that you have been mixed up yet again in some sordid affair."

Don't exaggerate. There haven't been that many.

"Oh no? As soon as you arrived you had nothing better to do than get involved with a militant of a banned party . . . "

Who? Saliou? That's not what he is in my eyes. And I don't know anything about his party. He never mentions it to me.

"What do you talk about then? They say he has fallen in love with you. That he'd like to take you as his second wife. But he is afraid of Oumou Hawa."

What contempt in his voice for this man who is afraid of his wife! No risk of that happening to him. She's tucked away in the North.

"I don't believe in friendship between a man and a woman. Except if he's a pederast like your colleague from the Institute."

This man is obnoxious. I am now fully aware of it. He's too sure of himself. He lacks sensitivity. I'm looking for a weak point and I've found it. Strange that he gave his sister to Saliou, despite the obvious discrepancies between them. He quickly corrects me. Too quickly, which means I hit home.

"Granted! I did everything I could to prevent the marriage. But he managed to get her pregnant. The Old Man was afraid of the scandal and accepted. Has he told you how one day my cousin Siradiou, who later married Ramatoulaye, Thierno, Oumou Hawa's fiancé, and I beat him up?"

Nothing to boast about! Three against one!

"He wasn't alone, but his colleagues ran away. Cowards, like himself."

Okay, don't let's get into an argument over Saliou. It's neither the time nor the place. And the discussion would be useless.

What I need to see life through rose-colored glasses is a good fuck.*
Not that I'm any different, mind you, from anybody else. But it is now
that it strikes me. The morning following these hours spent quietly at
Heremakhonon, I no longer tend to go halfway round the sun to meet
the moon, to think that my stay here is totally useless. Useless for
me, I mean. Even Amar counts for little. Becomes an unpleasant
memory and nothing more.

Pierre-Gilles, who knows nothing of the recent events and still
has memories of our inglorious escape from the Miami Club, is
surprised and shocked.

"It's a country without laws."

Well, let's say that the law is on the side of the strongest, with
less hypocrisy than elsewhere.

"We could perhaps try and see his wife. Help her."

In other words, wipe out our remorse with a few appropriate
words, smiles and a check. Especially a check. That goes without
saying! Since it's scarce, money cures everything in this country. An
expatriate colleague who ran over a girl's leg while driving his Ami 8
was surprised to hear himself blessed by the victim's father—he had
made out a check.

"Baké's bad! Worse than Mwalimwana!"

That's Alfa. It's like Amar's requiem. We start talking about other
things. Pierre-Gilles has just bought a balaphon: one of its original
features is . . . He gives a long, passionate explanation. All I can see
are little calabashes of different sizes tied together with reed and
fixed under irregular-sized strips of wood. Of course I like the sound
of the balaphon. He's also bought a Bambara statuette. Man seated,
hands on knees. Elongated trunk. Arms out of all proportion and very
slender. Thick-set legs, fairly big head. He still smells of Arden for
Men. What a pity!

Naturally, I have a class at the end of the morning. He too. But
lectures have become a boring formality while the students remain
utterly silent. I know what's behind their silence. I know what would

*In English in the original.

happen if there weren't soldiers at the door and the militia in the yard. Writing would reappear on the blackboard. The pigeon holes would fill up with leaflets. Mwalimwana's catechism would go up in flames under the mango trees. But am I paid to concern myself with the inner thoughts and desires of my students?

The town is taking on a festive air. Militia climbing up telegraph poles are hanging flags and colored bulbs. The children coming home from primary school watch with their mouths open. Armed with pitchforks, the soldiers in combat dress attack the rubbish piled up at street corners. Party offices are whitewashed. What's all this about?

The new director explains, shocked at our ignorance. Didn't we know that tomorrow is the anniversary of Mwalimwana's liberation? Mea culpa, mea culpa . . . Once upon a time, when the whites were here, the wicked fairy, who else but Mwalimwana (and a few others), working on the railways, staged the first national strike, which paralyzed freight shipments throughout the country. Naturally, the whites sent him and a few others to prison. So the people revolted, marched on the prison and they had to release the men they had ineptly made into heroes.

Alas! Mwalimwana's prison inmates (the new director shakes his head sadly) were demagogues and only too ready to seize power. This was proved on independence. Two went into exile in a country of opposition from where they slandered the regime. A third died of illness. May he rest in peace! The fourth? Ah, the fourth, he formed an opposition party that Mwalimwana in his goodness tolerated for a long time and then had to ban. Imprisoned at Samiana, he committed suicide. May he rest in peace, even so. The former director of the Institute, the sinister Saliou, was a member of the party which explains the agitation he caused among the students. That has all changed now. Students in Mao tunics sweep the yard, burn dead leaves and rake the alleys. The Institute has really changed since Saliou left. In other words, this country is like a green stagnant pond where the onlooker from the bank perceives nothing. You have to go down to the bottom to see the furious combats, the muffled blows, the fights to the death, moans and cries of victory. God preserve us from going down to the bottom.

So tomorrow (and the day after) is to be a paid holiday

throughout the country. Mwalimwana is to give a speech in the Place of the Martyrs. The schoolchildren, the soldiers and the militants will parade before him . . . I shall be a long way off. I have always hated such events. Perhaps because I paraded too much in a white dress around the Place de la Victoire, did formation movements, one/two, one/two under the indifferent and falsely benevolent eyes of some visiting prefect, sub-prefect, bishop or minister. Oh yes, I shall be a long way off.

Jean Lefevre and Adama have a little place on one of those small islands strung out at a stone's throw from the coast. They've offered me the key a hundred times. You get there by antiquated boat like the one to the Saintes. The sea is as blue as a child's drawing. The sky too. The sailor has blue eyes, a legacy of his Breton ancestors. Is it the present or the past? The present, the present. These two young scamps with their wide, roving eyes are Abdourahamane's children I'm taking with me. Their mother has knotted their spare boubou in a head-tie. I'm laden with enough provisions to cross the Sahel. Jean Lefevre and Adama accompany me to the wooden jetty whose rusty iron balustrades are eaten away by inedible shells. Pierre-Gilles and Alfa have promised me they will pay a visit.

Is it the present? Or is it the past? As a token of friendship.

We're being sent under Mabo Julie's supervision to Dr. Bageot, senator and mayor of Grand Bourg on the island of Marie Galante. I can remember a four-hour crossing on a rough sea. The air carries with it the smell of tar, asafoetida, vomit and salt that I have not smelled since. A child vomits overboard beside me. Black piglets squeal between passengers' feet. The jetty is rickety and studded with faded rubber tires. I'm lifted up like a packet into the arms of Mme Bageot, a frail little woman with a great reputation for kindness. It's the past. The past.

The inhabitants, curious to get a look at the visitors from the big island, come out of their low, green or pink wooden houses with their white-painted shutters. The women tie their madras in three knots. There are two flame trees in front of the church. At the foot of the great crucifix in the square lie blood-red petals. Dr. Bageot and his wife live in the finest house in the village. But I prefer the one opposite with its name in blue letters on a white enamel background. There's an ash-colored cat in a rather dark corridor. Mme Bageot picks him up in her arms; he snores like a pig. She points out his green eyes like a rattlesnake's. I cling to Mabo Julie who pushes me away from her. On the ground floor, sitting in a cane rocking chair, is an old woman whose eyes are covered by white specks, whose hair is yellowish grey like her wrinkled skin and whose breasts are big and sagging in a mauve checkered housecoat. My grandmother, who always terrified me, died the previous year and I seem to be seeing her again, alive, with that awful corpse smell in her clothes and her cold, horny hands over my face.

"Tala, cé plis piti là? Is this the youngest?"

I burst out crying. What a stay! I refuse to go near the old woman. I don't want to see the cat either. When Dr. Bageot, who has bad breath, tries to kiss us, I scream.

"Why are you being so naughty?" he asks. "Look at your sisters."

Just the thing not to say. My aversion for everything around me, born out of my childish fear of change, turns into hatred. I dream of killing, burning and putting an end to the old woman, my grandmother risen from the dead, *ad patres.*

When I return to La Pointe, I've lost four pounds. They grimly conclude that I, born on an island, must not like the sea. Because of me, we spent the next holidays in Saint Claude, at the foot of Soufrière. At least, that's what they say. I never believed it was because of me. They were looking for an excuse to parade themselves at Saint Claude, the mulatto stronghold where the Blacks used to walk on tiptoe, the Bakra having fled higher up. So we had our holiday at Saint Claude. We rented a villa from some hard-up mulattoes who had a bakery and patisserie at Trois Rivières where they now lived. And believe me it was total anonymity. Eighty miles from La Pointe where his name carried so much weight, the Mandingo marabout was a complete unknown. No giving one's respects, no visits and no advice lavished on attentive listeners out in the street. No pew at church. We sat with the common folk on rickety straw chairs and even if we put big money in the plate the lady who took the collection (I can see her now, a little mulatto woman with plaits two yards long, the eldest of a family who lived in a deep South style home at the entrance to the village down a palm-fringed drive) didn't even give us a look.

We were not intruders at Saint Claude. We simply did not exist. My mother, who was keen on walking, in vain wrapped her yard length choker around her neck, took shelter under a wide-brimmed hat and pushed us in front of her along a steep road that seemed to come hard up against the green, leafy mountain, a favorite refuge of the *Bête à Man Hibé,* you just could not hear our footsteps. Nor our voices. We did not exist. Out with it! Out with it! It was here that everything began. And not during this doll's baptism which I have already described and where I approached him for the first time. I lied. You always lie when you confess. There's nothing more deceitful than a confession.

It's here!

The clergy do good works, everyone knows that. So they flatter their patrons. The local parish priest became good friends with the Mandingo marabout and Marthe, my mother, who invited him round one afternoon for a glass of porto. My sisters' gift for the piano was unveiled. This not only got us officially invited to the local fête at the Anne-Marie Javouhey hall (freshly repainted for the occasion), but also got 'Duet by Aida and Jalla Mercier' printed on the program with two figures dancing the minuet. He had to show his gratitude for the donations somehow. And then in his Christian soul he must have thought he was working to bring niggers and mulattoes together, born enemies. I, the little girl with no talent for society, was put into a three flounce lace dress; my curly hair was vigorously brushed with a pink silk bow on top. Thus decked out I took my seat in the room and looked around me. They were not my people, I could feel it. Pretending to ignore me they despised me with all their might. Why? Because their black blood was so diluted, even non-existent, whereas mine swelled in my veins and circulated underground, secretly yet ever-present, in my plump, well-fed, well-cared for little eight year old body. I observed. All the women seemed more beautiful than my mother, who was just as well dressed, however, in raw silk and a capeline. I can remember it as if it were yesterday. They appeared lovelier because of their slightly coppery, slightly tanned skin, their soft wavy hair spared by the straightener, heated over coals and dipped—ssh!—in petroleum jelly. They seemed more attractive because they were light-skinned, possessing therefore what my mother lacked to be perfectly beautiful and to be worthy of appearing in this light, square room with its pastel colors. A little girl recited a poem on the stage. Her light-brown ringlets glinted in the sun and I desperately wanted to resemble her. To be this little girl. To be. To be. And yet I was ashamed. Ashamed of this desire that my whole education claimed to demolish. We have nothing to envy them, I was repeatedly told. Nothing? Then why imitate them? Imitate them up to a certain point? Imitate them, equal them, rival them, except on this point? It was beyond understanding. I was lost. In the midst of these gracious and despising faces. Gracious and hateful. To whom I was attracted, yet forced to hate.

That's when I knew that they too felt this secret desire and the shame of it and lied about it. To themselves and to me. This doll's baptism was merely a personal revenge. The achievement of a dream buried under years of education and instruction, which turned out to be strong and alive. I found myself back at the Anne-Marie Javouhey hall, but no longer at the back (the priest had done what he could). At the front. The chosen child, led up to the platform, decorated with a silver-starred blue cloth, by one of those little, green-eyed mulattoes who had so cruelly ignored me years before—when, sitting between my father and mother, my sisters finished their duet to the polite applause of the priest and other members of the clergy oozing with benevolence. They returned to their seats, heads held high as we were told to walk. Small revenge, you'll say, perpetrated in the shade of one of Aunt Paula's rooms. Outside the sun is scorching. The sea into which we'll plunge is blue. Like a child's drawing. Like the one around me. Fodé, the youngest of Abdourahmane's children, feels sick and vomits over the side of the boat. A fat woman, who smells of the sea, hands me a lemon and laughingly gestures what I ought to do with it.

"She's asking whether he's your child."

No, he's not mine.

First and small revenge. Let's go on to the second. Strange, the second smacks less of revenge. Oh no. No more lies. Let's get things straight. Smacks less of revenge? Yes. There's no doubt it was an escape. To which I hoped there would be no going back. Let them tear their eyes out. Gesticulate. Suffocate to death in their two square mile island. I'm far, far away. I'm in Paris.

Fodé leans his hard, round little head against my breast. Perhaps he'll remember this trip in ten years time. How will he see it then? And how will he remember me? The boat knocks against the jetty. Baskets, boxes and children are being hauled up. I hold my hand to a bare-chested man in a pair or very dirty, baggy trousers who laughs because a gust of wind blows my skirt over my head. The women even show off their panties.

Jean Lefevre and Adama's place is small and set among coconut palms. Almost washed by the sea. Oh we're going to enjoy ourselves here. Because there are times when you are glad to get away from everything. It's not the romantic idea of solitude—silence—far from city noises. No. But you've collected facts from the corners of your life, like a housewife picking up dust from under the furniture. And you want to get them out into the open.

First. Amar. If I'm unhappy and confused, it's because I'm not more so. Because I don't care a damn. Come and go, make love, chat. It's realizing my indifference. My cruelty.

Second. Birame III. Here we're getting deeper into guilt. I've been able to carry on as if nothing has happened because I have pretended to believe Ibrahima Sory. I have persuaded myself to believe him. I've bought my peace for the price of a lie. Since he's lying. Is he lying? This brings me back to Ibrahima Sory who in fact is at the center of everything. In the center of what? I've given up looking a long time ago. What was I looking for in fact? In the center of what? These children are tiresome! Fodé has cut himself on a shell. I open my first aid kit. He pushes away my hand with the cotton wool dabbed in white spirit and screams. I persist in thinking that this child, these children, are happier than I was as a child. They tell me they're in rags, that their father hires his services to a foreigner. They've never tasted strawberry-flavored yogurt. They hadn't discovered toys before I came. I know it's a useless argument and Fodé limps off and will not tell me whether he's less happy or happier. Because he doesn't know.

Small revenge indeed. A paltry flight. And what's the third? Oh no, I'm not going to start asking myself questions again?

The sea is blue like a child's drawing. And warm. Like a doe rabbit's belly. She puts her small, twitching nose between the holes in the metal wire and I look her straight in her red eyes. I'm the one who wants to blow the third affair out of all proportion. Me alone.

Now the children are fighting. I can hear their screams. How do they see this trip? How will I figure in their fantasies? Children load an object, an insignificant creature, with symbolism. Like me, Cecilia Theodoros. (Theodoros! They must have had a great time giving us those names). Stoned in the school yard. That was me, me. The part of me I hated. Strange that the second affair was by far the least important in its implications. Naturally it's the reason why I'm here, up to my neck in water, my feet brushing the sand. It should count for more, symbolically. It was the very opposite, however—purely an individual adventure. With a man who for me was not a white man. But certainly the closest of the three—a lover, a friend as well as a companion. I climb out of the water; the wind is getting cool and the children must be hungry.

Although he had promised, I wasn't counting on Pierre-Gilles' visit. Now here he is off the first boat. Isn't Alfa with him? No, Alfa isn't. Let's leave it at that. Everybody has his own problems, mine are enough for me. At this time, the town must be resounding with the rumble of tanks, the scraping of jeeps, the rolling of drums, the roar of planes and the hammering of heels. The dignitaries sitting around Mwalimwana must be sweating in their ceremonial garb. What a waste of energy! I've never understood parades. It seems the people like them. It makes them feel the power of their country. Afterwards they respect the authorities.

How peaceful it is on the island! I'm Man Friday or almost. A Friday to whom the West has nothing more to teach. Who has already been messed around with. Pierre-Gilles is dragging the children in colored rings away from the beach. It intrigues me how we will be remembered by these children. And what will become of them? Streetcleaners, steeped in dreams on a Paris pavement? I hope not. With the help of Mwalimwana, the country will get out of its rut and build hospitals, dispensaries, schools, roads, motorways and council housing. That's what we should hope for isn't it? What peace!

Shall I sum up my stay? No. No summing up. Anything but that. It would be positively negative—would plunge me into despair. Because, after all, what have I been doing all this time? Nothing of any importance. I haven't done anything, that's for sure. On my return I won't entertain my friends sitting in a circle in my living room. I shall have no masks to show off. No statuettes. No hunting trophies. No expeditions. No hikes. You may wonder whether I got my money's worth. My fare I mean. Although I didn't pay for it. What a farce! Me crying over a spoilt identity, that's it isn't it? I come here as a travelling salesman from Europe to spoil other identities. I'm the one who's fleeing the alienated of my native isle and I come to work on other alienations. That's it, isn't it? Yes it is. And so what? I have to earn my living. Yes, let's make it both defensive and weepy. What do you expect? I have to eat . . . If Pierre-Gilles doesn't watch out, he'll drown these kids. And we'll have another body on our hands. Yet another. Always this habit of dramatizing. Amar will do his month in the clink and return to Comarex to make or sell slippers. Birame III . . . Strange how I'm starting to think of Birame III again after having kept him at a distance for such a long time. I dreamed of him. Our first outing across the town when he acted as my guide and I hardly listened to him.

"History will judge him for all this blood."

He had said it with a straight face. Because he wasn't afraid of clichés. Cliché? What does that mean? That you are hardened, inured to major ideas and the words that translate them. That you are ashamed of them. That they embarrass you as much as the words virtue, chastity and virginity embarrass a whore. I must go and see the pretty little whore from the Alcatraz whom I saw again at the Miami Club. She must have things to tell me. Baké.

"What are you laughing at all by yourself?"

I'm not laughing. I'm not laughing. Or else I was forcing myself. Pierre-Gilles lies down on an orange bath towel. He says abruptly:

"Alfa's getting married."

Oh I see now! To Mariama? No, to a girl from his village who has been waiting for him for years. Oh well, all's well that ends well. He collected the dowry and as Pierre-Gilles was very generous, enough to buy a few pieces of furniture to make an impression in his mud hut. Do you feel bad about it? Are you suffering? It was the only way it could end. No, I refuse to get sentimental over a story of this sort. Like Saliou over Amar's. Saliou has been out of a job for three months now. What does he live on? How does he feed his wife and three children? And all the parasites? I suppose his friends, the other militants, help. How does his secret party work? Because it does work. Doesn't it? Of course. It organized the demonstration at the Matanko mosque. How do I know? I don't.

Poor Pierre-Gilles, all I can offer you is chilled grapefruit juice. You're not thinking of killing yourself again, are you? He shrugs his shoulders. The terrible thing with these ends of affairs is that you know that one day the suffering will come to an end. That you are surreptitiously imagining the next affair and already curious and impatient for it to happen. And that you are partly playing the comedy of unconsolable despair. I had tears in my eyes going up the stairway to the plane, but the thought of seeing Paris, the Eiffel Tower and the Invalides, which I had never seen, consoled me. However strange it may seem, I and my sisters had never seen Paris because the Mandingo marabout and Marthe could not be bothered with children during their cultural visits to the capital. And they always left us with Mabo Julie and a daily call from Dr. Carzavel and his wife. Don't think we had time to breathe when they were away. Mme Carzavel insisted on doing everything as if our parents were at home and bullied Mabo Julie. She would bristle in protest. Mme Carzavel would scream:

"I'll tell your master and mistress you lacked respect."

My parents' cultural visits always ended in catastrophe called back by telegrams, letters or phone calls. They had enough time, though, to bring us back armloads of presents. Perhaps I'm too hard on them. They mimicked because they hadn't been taught anything else. They were victims. Like me. Before me. Fodé puts his arms around my neck. His mother complains I spoil him. How can you do otherwise with children who are so deprived. I mean materially. And don't know it. Perhaps that's the key to their charm. Undemanding, quarrelsome and greedy like the other kids.

The morning stretches out. Languid and full of *far niente*. The taste of salt. The smell of the ocean. Life stands still. At least for us. Not for those in town whose buildings we can make out quite clearly. Mwalimwana must be giving his speech now. Saliou told me he tries to imitate Fidel Castro and gives endless speeches lasting four to five hours. As he speaks in French, the majority of his listeners don't understand a word and it's the party leaders who give the signal for the applause and political slogans. I suppose Ibrahima Sory is sitting on his right. Or on his left, next to his heart, just as inscrutable as always, waiting. And Saliou must be lost in the crowd. What is Saliou hoping for? He and his party colleagues. And me, what am I hoping for? Nothing, that much has been settled. I'm living an affair with a different scenario, that's all. Let's think of something else. What? Yes, what? I sit up on my elbow. The town looks lovely from a distance. White with a terrace of green to the left. Pierre-Gilles is motionless in the sun much to the amusement of the children. Fodé puts some suntan lotion on his body. It's obvious they think the whites are mad. At least Pierre-Gilles will have got a tan that will make all his friends pale with envy. I'll have nothing to tell. Nothing to show. The plane has landed at Le Raizet. What kind of car have they got now? They open the door and the smell hits me: citronella. First, citronella, then others I can't put a name to. Nine years!

"Tell us."

What?

I put the eggs in a blue enamel pot. The tomatoes are red on the Formica table. The women make them into piles and stand behind them with their babies at their breast. They smile when I go by. I've been here three months and I haven't got one step further. Further into what? An egg's broken, damn. Mabo Julie would have reproached me for not having put salt in the water. Her specialty was suckling pig with eggplant. We used to eat it on special occasions. On my parent's wedding anniversary, for instance. With all the 'first niggers.' Mabo Julie was complimented.

"Such a gift."

They envied us Mabo Julie. Sometimes mother lent her to friends for a ceremony. It's not surprising that the Mandingo marabout now has the gout. I've tried to be ashamed no longer. But it's another shame I have to deal with. A feeling of guilt which isn't exactly the same. I've really had it. Pierre-Gilles sits facing me peeling potatoes. Even so he's got guts. I'd have thought a break with Alfa would have knocked him out completely. He must be hurt, but he's holding up. Like Jean-Michel when I told him I was leaving for Africa. He even pretended to laugh.

"Going to look for your ancestors."

Basically it was that. Alas!

I didn't find my ancestors. Three and a half centuries have separated me from them. They didn't recognize me any more than I recognized them. All I found was a man with ancestors who's guarding them jealously for himself and wouldn't dream of sharing them with me. If we could swap childhoods, then there'd be no more Anne-Marie Javouhey hall. No more mulattoes putting on the master's shoes. Copying their big houses. Crushing you with their silence. No more nigger odor. No more zombies to exorcise. My father, an old ascetic masked in a white veil. My mother dyeing her feet with henna. Her lips as blue as indigo. The Whites? Uncircumcised dogs! Yes, but for that you need love.

We have lunch in the shade of an almond tree. My head is resting on Pierre-Gilles' chest. Miles away—he strokes my face. Aren't we being odious lying here on the beach? He sits up, making me move so that my head rolls down to his thighs.

"Why odious?"

Obviously, he can't understand me. I'm an ambiguous animal, half fish, half bird, a new style of bat. A false sister. A false foreigner. It would have to start all over again from the beginning. I got off to a bad start in this country. I should have become interested. Interested in what was going on around me. Try to understand . . . Could I? I could have perhaps, if I could have forgotten myself, but I couldn't. And damn it. Time has totally stopped. It's sitting on the top of a mangy baobab where birds are the color of ashes perched in silence.

We are leaving the wharf surrounded by a high green fence when we come up against a group of soldiers. Not nonchalant and laughing as they often are. But tough, hands on hips. Typical soldiers. One of them stops us:

"Your papers, please."

He must be joking. Does this man really imagine that I went to sea for two days with my identity card and resident's permit? You need one here, delivered by the Ministry for Foreign Affairs and surrendered on leaving the country. Apparently yes. Since he signals to another soldier who manly steps forward and orders:

"Follow me!"

Pierre-Gilles, who is more prudent than I am and consequently law-abiding, I mean with his papers on him, tries to intervene. The first soldier motions to him to be quiet and so he stays with Fodé and Sidiki between his knees holding the baskets and the wet bath towels, looking perfectly ridiculous. To add to the absurdity of the situation, Fodé starts to howl on seeing me manhandled so suddenly. What is going on? The port is surrounded by soldiers armed to the teeth. A small dark green van is waiting. A soldier makes me get in. Inside there are already two terrified boys and a young girl chewing unperturbedly on a stick. I have the right to know what's going on. This van has an awful smell of vomit. I've always been sensitive to smells. The soldier orders us to keep quiet.

If this was happening at another time I would laugh. I have got a sense of the ridiculous even so. But it's six o'clock in the morning; I'm tired by two days of sea. I would like to go home, have a bath and change. And I'm convinced I haven't done anything to deserve this treatment. The soldier is barely twenty with scars on his cheek. He closes the door repeating "silence."

Am I going to obey? The two young boys give me pleading looks. The young girl doesn't respond. You'd think she didn't see me get in. Through a kind of barred window I can see the wide avenue around the wharf, silent and deserted by the usual sellers of quinqueliba and margarine-smeared bread which makes up the dockers' breakfast. Something is going on. But what? A third soldier arrives pushing two adolescents in front of him. If that's all they could get! They climb into the van which starts off with such a jolt that we are thrown against each other.

I never thought that one day I would cross town in such a sad contraption. Ibrahima Sory's Mercedes is a long way off! The soldiers are everywhere. At street corners, where nobody seems to go near the water taps, lorries are drawn up. In the Place of the Martyrs still decorated with stands of greenery, where yesterday Mwalimwana and the dignitaries were seated along M. Gandhi avenue, recently renamed in honor of the apostle of non-violence. I have never seen so many soldiers even after the demonstration that failed the previous week. It's useless asking my companions; they are absolutely terrified. Except for the girl who continues to chew and spit out bits of wood right and left. It's amusing to gaze at the town through these bars. Talibés, like dusty sparrows, emerge from a courtyard and stop in their tracks. Are they going to be asked for their papers as well? A woman is standing on the edge of the pavement, her hand shielding her eyes. She is obviously reluctant to go on.

We approach the central police station. It's only a just retribution. A few days ago Amar was brought here because of me. Today it's my turn. I look at the enormous building, seven floors high. Seven floors of cops, doing what? Doing their sordid work called maintaining law and order. You need policemen I suppose. As my concierge used to say it takes all kinds to make a world. On the roof, a flag and television-like aerials. Another jolt and then a soldier opens the van door. We get out. Soldiers are guiding across the yard lines of prisoners similar to ours. Because we are prisoners. All terrified (except me). A man beside me is mumbling something incomprehensible which might be prayers. An Al Hadji somehow mixed up in all this twists his beads. Am I to blame if my companions' fear is not getting through to me? I merely find the joke in very bad taste. As usual, an enormous portrait of Mwalimwana in a Mao suit greets us in the vast, square entrance hall. We are made to sit down on white wooden benches placed parallel to the wall. How long is this game going to last?

I am not amused. I get up. A policeman standing at the end of the line shouts in my direction: "Sit down!"

I ignore him and open the first door at random along a light, paved corridor. I find myself in a small room where behind a desk stacked with files a policeman is reading the *Quotidien Unique* while picking his teeth. He looks up, surprised. The policeman who has just ordered me to sit down enters at the same time on my heels. He starts shouting. I interrupt him, arrogantly declaring that I want to speak to the Minister for the Defense and the Interior. The policeman sitting down stares at me obviously hesitating between the desire to laugh at my claim and the fear that it might be well founded. I become a different person and repeat with an intensified arrogance, which I didn't think myself capable of, that I will not wait any longer. He decides to get up and go out, leaving me in the protection of his colleague who is somewhat at a loss. In a way, I'm ashamed of myself. But why? I'm not going to stay in this hall and take part in such an absurd, unamusing game. On the wall there is a photo of Mwalimwana, same model but in miniature. In a corner there is also a revolving fan that grates.

The door opens. This time it's a police officer in a peaked hat. He stares at me, then decides to ask me my name. It's very obvious he is afraid of making a blunder. He disappears. How did it go for Amar a few days ago? He must have protested that he was innocent; just drank one or two glasses too many. Where is he now? The officer reappears with two other policemen. Without a word they accompany me into a bigger room where there are two armchairs. I sit down. They disappear. I have never been so close to cops. Thank goodness the Mandingo marabout who openly called himself an anarchist did not frequent their presence. He used to rage against the state, while accepting the Legion of Honor and the Cross of goodness knows what.

How long am I going to stay in this room? I go over to the window and see the yard swarming with people. I mean policemen, soldiers, men and young people. Few women. All this agitation seems hardly credible. I can't take it seriously. The door opens and Ibrahima Sory's chauffeur rushes in, this time surrounded by five men, one of whom is a corpulent officer with a simpleton's face. Oh no excuses! Can I just know what is going on? And why have I been subjected to this treatment? This treatment, don't let's exaggerate. The whole affair won't have lasted an hour and nobody has been disrespectful. Respect! Have I deserved respect? Now I've started to talk like my mother who swore by the word. To hear her she never got enough respect. An officer decides to answer my questions. Obviously I couldn't have known anything from my island of Kariba. The day before a time bomb had been placed along the road Mwalimwana was to take to the Place of the Martyrs. Fortunately, something went wrong and the bomb exploded too late killing three party dignitaries and men and women in the crowd massed along the streets. Three days of national mourning were declared in honor of the martyrs as well as a state of emergency. The men behind the killings have to be found. Well congratulations! I'd never have thought the opposition was so well organized. In fact, I never even believed in the opposition. What was it made up of? Chatterboxes like Saliou, secretive people like Yehogul? Suddenly it all becomes real.

I retrace my steps across the hall, this time accompanied by the chauffeur and the two almost fawning officers. My companions of misfortune are still sitting on their wooden benches. I can't manage to catch their eye. They don't seem to recognize me. The Mercedes is waiting in the yard. An officer opens the door and just then I see Saliou. Saliou between two policemen with his hands in his boubou pockets as if he were strolling. Saliou! He has the nerve to laugh taking my hands in his.

"It seems these gentlemen have a few questions to ask me. But what are you doing here?"

Yes, it's me he's talking to! The policemen look at us surprised, ready I imagine to think twice about me as it's obvious I have very bad acquaintances.

"I'll be alright. Don't take it so seriously."

He brushes my cheek as if I were a child and goes off. Before entering the building he turns round and gives me a wicked wink. What can I do? Nothing. I can't do anything. I get into the car.

Frankly, I was not prepared for events of this sort. I'm stupefied, stunned. Yesterday I was swimming in an indigo sea. I was playing with children. I was playing around with Pierre-Gilles, half out of fun, half out of desire. Because there's nothing more irritating than a good-looking homosexual. And this morning I'm plunged into drama, because there are no other words for it despite my terror of superlatives. It's really and truly a drama. And I can't believe it. Like someone you have to wake up with a pinch. Who screams in pain at the sight of blood. The soldiers have cordoned off the town. It's a big game. All this seems especially uncalled for as the people appear so inoffensive. Defenseless. The jobless start to line up at the labor exchange. The women decide to go to market. Or am I mistaken? Are they hiding their force under a façade of passivity and fatalism? That's what I get for having wanted to keep out of things. Incapable of having an opinion. The Mercedes leaves town. Oh no! I want to go home. The chauffeur shakes his head vigorously: the master's orders. He wants to see me. Oh, I can imagine what he has to say. Not funny for a minister to be called at dawn because his mistress has been found without identity papers. Mistress? We should invent another word. This one isn't suitable.

The agitation in town has not reached the residential areas. Except that Mwalimwana's villa has had its guard doubled. So they tried to kill him the day before. Or is it just an excuse to weed out a few troublemakers?

With drought and famine in the villages the false prophets would have a difficult time. So they have to get a headstart. The gates of Heremakhonon open. The master receives me in his office hurriedly vacated by a secretary. I sink into an armchair as I suddenly realize I'm tired. Very tired.

"Veronica, what were you doing?"

No, no pretending. You know full well that I don't meddle with your private schemes. And I'm not one of those who wanted to send Mwalimwana *ad patres.*

"We have proof that a boat had tied up loaded with mercenaries waiting for the death of Mwalimwana before entering town to take over power. Now you arrived by boat . . . "

Let's not be ridiculous! I want to go home if that's all you've got to say.

"I would rather you stayed here . . . as long as the situation in town remains confused."

I should be grateful to him: it's proof he is concerned about me. Unfortunately, I am too tired to thank him. I get up. He remains seated behind his desk. Does he really believe in what he has just said? Does he believe in his insinuations? This is all quite absurd. Saliou, Saliou, what are they going to do with Saliou? I can't pronounce his name, make enquiries about him. I don't know why. Out of fear. Fear of opening up a wound? Fear of releasing anxiety and anguish? They are there nevertheless. What am I going to do? Stay at Heremakhonon? Well, for the time being. I leave the office and bump into the secretary. Perhaps he was listening behind the door like all good secretaries. He looks at me out of curiousity—and lust. What must be going through his head!

I have nothing better to do for the time being than to retreat to the room which has more or less ended up becoming my room and where Abdoulaye has faithfully refilled the flower vases. Today it's roses. I sit on the edge of the bath. The tap is on full-blast, I don't hear the door open and suddenly I see him behind me dressed in a Mao suit, probably more appropriate for the present circumstances than his sumptuous ceremonial boubous. For the first time since our strange relationship began he does not seem in complete control. He's tense, worried.

"You don't realize the seriousness of what's going on in town. I am asking you to stay here."

Well, hasn't the order already been given?

"There is no question of an order. If there were, you would promptly disobey it."

The remark takes me by surprise. I have never shown any sign of having an independent mind. On the contrary. He looks at his watch and I understand he desires me, but is thinking of his chauffeur and secretary who are waiting for him in the garden and no doubt muttering some dirty joke at his expense.

"The Minister is having a good time. When things are going so badly."

Are things going so badly? That's what I can't manage to make out. I saw truckloads of soldiers, guns, all the trappings of violence. But I haven't seen the enemy. Where is he? Where is he hiding? Or is it the people with bare hands whose face I am unable to decipher? Behind a mask? Who can tell me? Do I need anybody to tell me? Couldn't I try to figure it out myself? Make my little personal investigation like an American private detective operating off the beaten track. Is it too late? Why should it be too late? At the same time I too desire him and I'm not worried about a chauffeur or a secretary waiting for me. Nor about the affairs of state. Yes, I desire him. Perhaps because the stupid affair at the main police station shook me more than I realize, perhaps because an affirmative response from him would console my malaise, I mean my shame, at the desire I'm feeling at the present moment. I put the inevitable question to him which up until now common sense has outlawed— do you love me?

He utters a sigh that I prefer not to analyze and replies somewhat impatiently:

"Love is not something you chatter about."

Well, that's a good one! And what about all the poems, the songs and novels on the subject. All that literature that goes back to the beginning of mankind and continues to flourish year after year to the delight of silly schoolgirls and others. Love is certainly the most talked about subject. You might say it's the only subject talked about. He laughs. He has fine, white teeth, a little irregular, with sharp canines a little too small.

"One thing is certain, Veronica, there's no getting bored with you."

Once again this remark takes me by surprise. So I amuse him! I always thought myself melancholy, not entertaining in the least. He kisses me like a man who has wasted enough time. Cataclysms and catastrophes heighten desire, it's a well-known fact. Torrential rain, a raging storm, hurricanes, fires or in the present case, political turbulence. I grip his shoulders which are wet with sweat. At the same time under my eyelids I can see . . . Saliou laughing in the courtyard of the central police station. It's like a film going round and round in my head which prevents me from neither experiencing pleasure. Nor coming. Nor starting a second time. It's horrible. I would like to interrupt the film, but I can't. Stop myself from experiencing so much pleasure, but I can't. The conflicting images and sensations come together, magnified to exaggeration until I want to die or I die. He moves aside and looks at his watch again.

"They'll never understand why I'm late today of all days."

Who are 'they'? They don't exist. He sits on the edge of the bed and asks me the same question which seems so extraordinary when he says it: "And you, do you love me?"

Me? I imagine that I love you which comes down to the same thing. He doesn't laugh, surprisingly enough. On the contrary, he seems pensive. Then, as if to make the most of the situation and thereby stifle his scruples (he must have some even if they aren't the same as mine) he returns to me. This time the film is different. A helicopter roars over a field. The grass is flattened. At the controls there is a man whose face I can't make out but who terrifies me, I don't know why. Who gets ready to jump from his helicopter to devour me like a beast, wringing from me a cry of pain. A single cry, prolonged like a wail.

The chauffeur and the secretary must have got through quite a few jokes by now. They must have even begged Abdoulaye to intervene discreetly, to recall the Minister to his duties. The Minister makes no move to leave.

"Promise me you won't go out. We are burying the victims of the attack this afternoon. We are afraid they will try again."

They would really have a nerve. With all this display of force in the streets. Real kamikazes! Or else they are sure of inside help from the police or the army. He doesn't answer, gets dressed in silence, looks at his watch and whistles between his teeth. I have inflicted a defeat on Mwalimwana in my fashion.

I remain alone in the room where the air conditioning is on full blast and the roses smell of a mortuary. If I had any pride left I'd go into town. Oh, of course, I'll come back to Heremakhonon. I shan't be away for long. Heremakhonon and Ibrahima Sory are traps I couldn't avoid, even if I wanted to. But I don't want to. Abdoulaye begs me to stay:

"There are lots of police and soldiers in town."

Rest assured. I have no intention of defying anyone. He follows me to the gate and watches me go off, helpless. Sometimes fate is on your side. Duly enrolled by the leaders of each section, the militants of the neighboring villages are on the march and a line of trucks, bicycles, taxis and vehicles of all sorts surges towards town; men, women and children waving flags and pennants are packed in like sardines singing the Party songs. Those who haven't found room in a vehicle go on foot, the women dressed in white, the color of mourning, with tricolor headties and the children in their school uniforms. The musicians make a lot of noise and the atmosphere seems curiously more conducive to a celebration than to sorrow and mourning.

I realize it's a not very subtle referendum Mwalimwana wishes to organize. Let the crowd attending the ceremony show its affection, its horror at yesterday's attack and renew its confidence in him by its mere presence. I'm walking beside a woman with a child on her back who motions to me to seek shelter under her parasol. In front of us there are two comrades who can't stop laughing. She points her chin at them in reproach. At the entrance to the town there's an enormous jam. Vehicles merge from all directions. Soldiers are directing the crowd, they have recovered their good humor and are exchanging jokes. Nobody pays any attention to me when on reaching the Den Bata mosque I turn off into a deserted street. I must reassure myself that nothing has happened to Saliou.

He is at home, eating a late lunch which is not very copious. Oumou Hawa and the baby have left the hospital and are sleeping in the room next door.

"Now, now, what did you expect to happen to me? You must understand that all this is a gigantic farce designed to cover up the real problems. The people are dissatisfied and the students angry."

Oh dear, he's going to make a speech. Illogical as ever, after having wanted instruction, I reject it. It's because I distrust Saliou. He offers a ready-made vision, his own, ready-made answers. I cling to my objectivity. My wretched objectivity. He calls it a farce. Even so, six men died. Six innocent victims. He shrugs his shoulders.

"How many men have died since independence? Innocent victims as you say? And without national honors, in complete anonymity or covered in shame."

There is a certain callousness in Saliou. But this is no time to quarrel. What a relief to see him sitting there safe and sound. He smiles teasingly.

"I didn't know you liked me to that extent."

To what extent? Perhaps I like him too much to love him. He's too close, too familiar.

I could have made his acquaintance in a lecture room at the Sorbonne, at some left-wing student meeting where I had wandered in or on some railway station looking for the right track. Saliou is an African, a man from Africa, but not my Africa and consequently does not crystallize the love I am seeking for myself through her. Am I making myself clear? No . . .

"Now that you've seen me alive, please go home. Don't come out again."

Why? Are he and his comrades plotting something? Well, how do I know whether he is not mixed up in this somber assassination attempt? He raises his eyes to the heavens.

"I told you it's a farce."

The word farce I repeat seems to be inappropriate. But let's not spoil the euphoria of the moment. Since it is almost euphoric. Seeing him there, on the other side of the table. Oumou Hawa comes out of the bedroom visibly calmed. They interrogated him for three hours and searched the entire house. She must have been through some unpleasantries. I stroke the little shaved head of the baby. Saliou literally pushes me outside. I can face the town. I walk light-footed through the streets. The entire town is concentrated along the main arteries, one running from the Matanko mosque, an enormous inelegant building (the pride of the town nevertheless) to the Place of the Martyrs and the other from the National Pary Headquarters modelled on the People's Palace in Warsaw (why Warsaw I don't know) to the central market. The noise of the crowd and the din of the musical instruments reach me over the low roofs of the huts along with the wail of the sirens—the men in power on the move.

Surprise, surprise! Pierre-Gilles, Abdourahmane, his wives, a few expatriate colleagues, Adama and Jean Lefevre are worrying themselves to death in my living room. They greet me like a person miraculously cured at Lourdes who has picked up his bed and walked, and tell me they were about to notify the embassy. About what, good heavens! My disappearance! Yes, I'm an irresponsible person with no sense of danger. Like the girl born with no sense of touch whose parents lived in terror. My disappearance. I didn't think one minute anybody would worry about me. Are they mad? Or am I? Me, probably. Adama is crying genuine tears in a corner of her handkerchief.

"If you knew how worried I was."

I am besieged with questions. I can't exactly recount what I was doing most of the morning. I have always lied very badly, especially to myself. But I have to this time. Make up a credible story as best I can. How easy it would be to paint myself as a heroine, her honor and virtue spoiled, raped and tortured. Besides, that's what they expect from me and I disappoint everyone. Jean Lefevre is frankly sceptical:

"Those bastards behaved themselves?"

Yes they did. Only Pierre-Gilles senses a lie and looks at me out of the corner of his eye. I'll tell him all about it later on and we'll have a laugh. To sum it up, what for millions of individuals is a national tragedy, has plunged six families into mourning and thousands of others into terror is for us an excuse for amusement. The men and women I saw picked up this morning and file across the police station yard were not laughing. Even Saliou's laugh must be forced. Who laughs in front of a gun? Only those of our species. Oh well, all's well that ends well. I am home. My friends are real friends, they have proved it. Now go home in turn; the hour is unsafe. You can hear a strange crackling in the air. Adama and Jean climb into their car.

Pierre-Gilles is convinced that my deliverance merits opening one of the half bottles of champagne he keeps permanently in his fridge. Yes, let's drink; why not? A young man is sweeping the terrace of his villa. Thin, his head shaved very closely, a deep look of contempt. He comes and goes with his brush between his hands like the reins of a well-trained horse.

"A beauty isn't he?"

You can say that again! It's no exaggeration. And who is this beauty? It's Alfa's young brother from the village who has been obligingly handed over to the former master. I suppose the wages and the functions are the same? Pierre-Gilles, I'm not that moral, but sickened. Oh just as much by myself as by you since we are both in the same boat. OK, I don't practice sodomy, but I prostitute to my desires what I'm unable to obtain. Fortunately, I don't obtain much. Neither do you when it comes down to it. Bodies that will tire of ours, escape and leave not a trace. Not a trace? Pierre-Gilles laughs gaily while uncorking the bottle. He has greenish-blue eyes which are accentuated even more as his face gets browner. Black curly hair. I don't know what impulse seizes me, but I kiss him violently. No, I know what impulse. A desire to humiliate him, in other words humiliate myself through him. In the same way I imagine men must possess a whore. Or, at the other end of the scale, stuck-up women used to having their own way. A desire to hurt him, i.e. me. To degrade us to goodness knows what level. He of course interprets the matter quite differently.

"Veronica, are you doing me the honor of being jealous?"

Perhaps. I sit down on a sofa covered with a thick woven blanket from Mali. Blues and orange dominate. He fills our two glasses.

"We ought to try. One of my friends has a theory that only a black woman can interest a homosexual in women."

We poor negresses! For centuries we have been satisfying the shameful desires of the white male. Now they've put us with the perverts as well! The theory is worth elaborating.

"According to him black is a virile color."

Well, I never! After all the theory is no more absurd than any other. No more absurd than a good many others circulating on our account. The young man has finished sweeping the terrace, comes in and turns on the radio without as much as a glance. Apparently he's interested in what's going on in town. In a resounding voice,

Mwalimwana is tracing the career of one of the victims:

"By dint of perseverance, intelligence and humility, Comrade Sansiba, a genuine child of the people, the guardian of virtue . . . "

OK, OK, it's not for us. There's no reason why we should listen to it. Pierre-Gilles takes me back to Heremakhonon. That's where I feel best. Most of the streets have been closed to traffic. Soldiers are on duty at a crossroad. One of them stops us. We are scrupulously in order, I've learned my lesson, but this soldier is out for trouble. The revolver on his hip and the gun over his shoulder have gone to his head. True, let's be fair, we must look very suspicious, overexcited as we are on a day of national mourning. He insists:

"Where are you going?"

Pierre-Gilles goes bland and explains we are going to the beach. It's not forbidden to go to the beach, is it? The soldier stares at me. Yes, it's me he's staring at, full of contempt. Contempt for this black woman who is turning her back on the town to go and play around with a white man. Contempt from this side, contempt from the other. For radically opposite reasons of course. And it's not me they despise. But the image they get of me and their interpretation. Erroneous and corny! We glare at each other. How he'd like to send me to rot in some jail. Fortunately he can't. He goes three times round the car, kicks the front right wheel as if to make sure it's in good condition and finally resigns himself to letting us go.

"Did he think he frightened me? I've a grandfather who's a general."

Pierre-Gilles whistles while he drives at breakneck speed along the straight, deserted road bordered with cotton trees and baobabs. He seems content.

The most illogical thing is that once I get to Heremakhonon I don't know what to do with myself. I listen over and over again to music from Burundi, solemn, funereal and beautiful. I read. I wait in other words. For when I become Marilisse. All things considered, I haven't stopped embodying a series of mishaps. Is this one the least despicable? Abdoulaye comes up.

"The town's on fire."

On fire?

The darkening sky deepens the red of the flame trees which

disappear into the thickening shadows. The servants come out of their quarters; Ibrahima Sory's younger brothers out of their room; Ramatoulaye's little servants have jumped over the hedge and everyone is asking questions with their nose in the air. One of the cook's sons perched in a tree excitedly describes everything he sees. He can't see much more than we can, however—smoke and blood-soaked trails of cloud. For the first time I'm afraid. Not for myself. I feel protected. Not for myself? And suppose we were the ones under attack, I mean the inhabitants of this district whose luxury is an insult to the town's poverty. Mwalimwana and his guards, everyone. And suppose the crowd, whom I thought obedient and disciplined, turned round under cover of night and marched on us with sticks and stones? Oh, I'm off again. What can be going on? Perhaps the town is a furnace. Where human flesh is roasting. Where hair and nails crackle and spread their frightful odor. There is a voluptuousness in exaggerating fear. Like a child who is convinced he hears the voice of *Maman de Leau.* His terror is stifled in the perfumed skirts of his nurse. I haven't got anyone to console me. Just an empty bed where I shall end up sleeping. The horsemen of Burundi gallop softly in the background. You always end up going to sleep. I don't think fear can keep you awake for hours. You go under without noticing; the bright light is a challenge to open eyes. I go out into the garden. A houseboy is washing down the terrace. Does he know what burned down last night? He is embarrassed because I've asked him a question and he doesn't know what to reply. Abdoulaye emerges and explains they burned down the Party Headquarters and tried to take over the radio station. Things are getting worse. Who are "they"? Abdoulaye keeps his eyes down, groping for his words in this foreign language which creates yet another barrier between us.

"Those who don't like Mwalimwana!"

Are there a lot like them? He thinks again and manages to say: "They say there are."

I'm starting to conduct my little private investigation. It's time the town was put to the fire and sword. Fire and sword? I leap over the hedge that separates us from Ramatoulaye's. Her servants are sitting on little wooden benches tackling an enormous mound of washing. The soap froths over their arms. They smile at me. I never know on which leg to stand. Sometimes they smile and greet me with kindness. Sometimes with contempt and hatred. Whereas I am always the same, I don't change. As if they look at me through deforming prisms which take no account of my real nature. Ramatoulaye is in bed. She didn't sleep a wink all night as her husband hasn't come home. They set fire then to . . . Yes, I know. Who are "they"? She has told me once, hasn't she? The Socialists, the Marxists! It's all the same, isn't it? She's already told me, hasn't she? Mwalimwana wanted to plant the tree of Socialism and then realized what fruit he was collecting. So he's trying to uproot it, but it's probably too late. Are there a lot of Socialists and Marxists? She lifts up her arms. That's all there are! The servants are Marxist, the cooks and cripples at the market. It's like a gangrene. How much of this can I believe? I'll never manage to make my investigation. The first thing I believe in such cases is to choose one's interviewees very carefully. It's called sampling. All my interviewees belong to the same camp, Abdoulaye, Minister's houseboy, Ramatoulaye, Minister's wife. All the same or virtually. Then there is Saliou and Yehogul and I don't want to listen to them. Is that my objectivity? I leap back over the hedge. The master has returned. The chauffeur is washing the Mercedes which is probably the apple of his eye.

However strange and improbable it may seem I have never entered Ibrahima Sory's room. I think today's exceptional circumstances authorize it. He is lying on his very low bed and Abdoulaye is kneeling down massaging him with probably more skill than I would. He smiles on seeing me enter. This surprises me. I expected a frown or a scolding like the Mandingo marabout's when I entered his Holy of Holies library, wall to wall with books, the bottom shelves holding the *Encyclopédie Quillet,* Gibbon's *Decline and Fall of the Roman Empire* and other leather-bound tomes I can still smell. I was only interested in the upper shelves containing *Remembrance of Things Past* and its mysterious titles, Sodom and Gomorrah, two biblical towns whose description I searched in vain through the chapters, surprised instead to find a succession of duchesses and princes whose lives did not interest me at all. Then there was the formidable series by Zola, formidable because the titles, *L'Assommoir, Germinal, Le Ventre de Paris* and *La Bête Humaine* evoked a terrifying violence in my ten-year old mind. He smiles at me, says a few brief words to Abdoulaye who retires, hands me the little gourd whose peppery perfume I haven't forgotten and lets himself go for a few moments.

"You massage very badly, Veronica!"

One does what one can. You were in the thick of the action, why don't you tell me what happened last night? He closes his eyes.

"You already know. They burned down the Party Headquarters and took over the radio station. What they hoped to do by such madness, I don't know."

They! Always them! Who are they? Where are they hiding? How do they communicate? It's like an army battling against invisible creatures that sound hollow when struck. He opens his eyes.

"Tell me, that pederast who's your neighbor, is he interested in women now?"

Mr. Minister, are you doing me the honor of being jealous? And at such a moment when you are in the thick of a struggle against the enemies of your fatherland. That's what it is, isn't it?

"All men are jealous. It's a natural sentiment."

Jealous! Possessive to be precise. A cartoonist illustrated it: My car—my garden—my house—my swimming pool—my wife. And the other replies: My arse.

He sits up.

"And that white man who was your lover in Paris you told me about, do you write to him?"

Well I didn't expect this sort of conversation this morning! I've been trying for weeks to get him interested in something other than the shape of my hips or my breasts. Well, I try! I don't quite know how to go about it . . . Whether I write to Jean Michel? He's the only person I write to. I imagine him reading my letters in the street, at red lights making the other drivers furious; he already drives so badly. Like a poet he says. Although he's never written a line, even at sixteen, so he says.

"I wonder how one can love a white man. After all they did to us . . . For me, only whores should deal with white men."

It's obvious he's not exactly thinking of me. It's a thought. Or perhaps in his jealousy, let's say retrospective jealousy, he is trying to destroy, despoil a part of me that escapes him. But I am deaf to the word he used. I don't want to hear. Whore? Does he know because of him, yes him, lying on his low bed, me massaging him as best I can, forty students who had begun to like me, yes like me, I can remember their welcome, their first questions to a sister from abroad, lost and found like the prodigal son, called me that? And not in words that vanish into thin air. In writing on the blackboard, in capital letters in red chalk.

"Why didn't you ever tell me?"

What would you have done? Sent your soldiers into the Institute again to terrorize defenseless children, take away the bravest, have them recite a concocted self-criticism on a platform decorated with the national flag, make them tar the roads in the North and kill them like you killed Birame III? You killed him, didn't you. Stop lying.

"Lying!"

He slaps me. A resounding, burning slap. Nobody has ever slapped me before. Never, not even the Mandingo marabout and Marthe, my mother, who had their own ideas on bringing up children: one, that there was too much corporal punishment to their liking in the West Indies and, secondly, that a firm scolding should suffice. Never even Mabo Julie whom I used to drive mad in the kitchen. Never even a schoolmistress who would not have dared touch one of Mr. Mercier's children out of fear of being brought before the disciplinary council and incurring a reprimand. At the most, a rough word from one of my sisters who were not inclined to violence, but rather to playing peacefully with their dolls. It's not pain. It's stupefaction. Before the fury. The fury of not having some weapon within reach, like one of those sharp arrows that decorate Pierre-Gilles' living room that I could plunge into his breast. The blood spurts. In all my life, I have never felt so violently the desire to kill.

I find myself outside, the sun reflecting off the Mercedes that the chauffeur is polishing. I probably have such an awful face that he abandons his shammy and takes to the wheel, racing the engine into fourth and speeding off with me towards town. Pierre-Gilles is in bed. What a lot of half-naked individuals I've seen in bed since this morning. He watches me approach with genuine terror. Like a peasant quietly in his field who watches Betsy or Flora bear down on him. He strokes me and listens with interest. That's his feminine side:

he loves little incidents then shrugs his shoulders.

"I've never understood what you saw in that man. I saw him at a reception at the President's palace. Good-looking, perhaps, but arrogant, insincere and cruel."

Suddenly he sits up and lets go of me.

"They've arrested your friend Saliou."

Arrested!

"Passeron had the wonderful idea of taking some street pictures and got nicked by the soldiers. He saw Saliou being taken out of a van, handcuffed and dusted up."

Handcuffed? Dusted up? Pierre-Gilles begs me in vain to keep calm and repeats that I can't do anything, but I don't pay any attention.

The street is deserted. Not a child on his way to school; not a houseboy going to market; the shuttered houses seem empty of their inhabitants. At a corner, a group of soldiers, one of them holding a machine gun, but seemingly inoffensive. I decide to take matters in hand. I go forward and explain I am looking for a doctor.

"A doctor!"

They look at each other. Really what an idea to be ill on such a day! One of them, very young, shyly hazards a question:

"For you?"

I explain it's my baby who has had diarrhea all night. They look more and more embarrassed. Finally, one makes up his mind.

"Go down the street to the end, turn right, there's a doctor there. If they stop you, say Leopard III let you through."

Leopard III! I'd laugh if it weren't so tragic. I go down the street and turn right looking for my way in this ghost town. I arrive in sight of Saliou's house. It's guarded by soldiers. What am I going to do now? What's the use of going further? Of asking questions? All that I'll get is a few hours at the main police station and perhaps Ibrahima Sory won't feel like releasing me so quickly after this morning's little scene. There I am. I hesitate. I'm frightened, yes frightened, when I hear an enormous rumbling, as if a giant tree were being felled in a nearby forest. A muffled voice calls out behind me:

"Sister, sister!"

A door half opens, I'm snatched from behind and find myself in a dark, square little room. A young woman is sitting on an un-comfortable-looking bed holding a sleeping baby in her arms; another child is playing obviously on the ground with cardboard boxes. The man who forced me in, and a young boy, have their eyes glued to the chinks of the door which is now closed, and motion to me to be quiet. I go up and put my eyes to the rough wood; the noise gets louder and becomes deafening. And then I see a tank advancing. A tank, the latest product of American or Russian technology, it doesn't matter which, in the narrow, rutted road, bordered with mud huts or modest concrete houses. This poor little town of under three hundred thousand inhabitants, most of whom have great difficulty feeding themselves, walk untiringly under the sun and are sceptical that man has made it to the moon.

The tank, gun pointed, moves on. A terrifying death machine that men of another continent made and sell. Like they first sold pearls and mirrors. Then rusty guns. Before sending their missionaries, their priests, their teachers such as I who have nothing to criticize, but suddenly am tired and fed up with it all. The worse of all in such moments is the feeling of helplessness. I can do nothing. Saliou has been arrested. I don't know where Oumou Hawa is. Yehogul could tell me if he has not already been arrested. He must be in a very tight situation too. I'll have to wait then. Wait for what? For time to go by. The radio only broadcasts military music. Afternoon, is it the afternoon? Abdourahmane tells me that Mwalimwana is to address the nation over the radio.

Political eloquence has always seemed abject to me. Since the beginning of time, men, leaders, have climbed platforms and promised wonders to others. They don't believe a word of it. I know there were a few idealists, cranks who did believe. Whether they believed or not they were unable to keep their promises. Otherwise we wouldn't be where we are. Some in opulence, others in shit. I know I ought to shut up since I've always refused to take sides. But what would my "engagement", as they say, have changed? Not much. Nothing. I listen to Mwalimwana in the hope of deciphering a message, an intention, from the hollow, overworked phrases. Like the racing forecast. Except that it's the fate of a friend. And the punters of the Prix de l'Amérique have never been so worked up as I am. Mwalimwana speaks for three hours. More, as I can't bear it and turn the knob. What shall I do? Wait. The day will come to an end sooner or later. Night too. Then there'll be another day. And what will that bring? We don't know yet. We can dream. The doors of the camp open. The wound on Saliou's forehead has healed. Nothing more than a pink, washed-out scar soon covered over by his black skin. He is carrying a bundle of clothes. He limps as they beat him up quite a bit. Oumou Hawa will massage him. Me too. Tomorrow. When tomorrow comes.

The night sets in. It has never been so quiet. Even the muezzin withholds his call as if the echo terrifies him. There is a noise in the compound. Very slightly. A Mercedes—these sleek animals run smoothly. Ibrahima Sory has never come to my house before. He has always left his chauffeur to come and get me. I ought to be flattered to see him here. It's a victory. A small victory in fact, like the previous one, that occurs when I'm no longer interested. When I'm no longer interested? Let's not pretend. Whatever is happening outside, whatever my concern for Saliou, nothing is more important than this man standing at the half-open door with the night and the silence behind him. They'll say I got excited. It's easy for the intelligence to break down a feeling, to reduce it to pieces that are absurd, even shocking in the light of reason and common sense. The feeling is there, however. Its violence and power to make us suffer have not dwindled. Ibrahima Sory closes the door carefully.

"I'm going to give you proof that this Birame III you are so interested in is alive."

Proof?

"Yes, I'll have a pass made out for you and you can go and see him and his companions at Tellubery. You'll see I never lie."

I suppose I've hurt him. Does he think I'm going to apologize? Because I could make things difficult as well. Haggle. Ask what Birame III has done to deserve such treatment. Why have they kept him in a camp for weeks like a criminal? Alas! I'm beginning to realize that it is already so wonderful for him to be alive that I consider myself satisfied. Oh, I'd love to talk of Saliou. But I feel he has capitulated on one point, two, if we count him being at my house, and he shouldn't be pushed any further. Yet this silence is an unjustifiable treason.

"Are you coming with me?"

It must cost him a lot to say that. Why does he say it then? Because he likes making love to me. And in his male pride he does not want to leave me the initiative of making the break. He means to possess me until saturated with a few concessions here and there. I have no illusions on that point. If I were a flirt, I'd act up and make him beg for me. All these little intrigues are not worth it, and if I don't follow him I shall have to confront the night alone. Alone until the sun comes up.

The town is dead. Even the homeless have deserted the market where they usually shelter and have taken refuge at a relative's who will not turn them out in these troubled times. Dogs scuttle in front of the car's headlights. There are armed patrols. I accept his silence because there is nothing to say. To be more exact, I've understood there is nothing we can say that doesn't end up dividing us. And the only form of dialogue is the one that satisfies him, whereas I consider it inadequate, even despicable in my Westernized infantilism. Trucks loaded with soldiers literally bar the vicinity of Mwalimwana's villa. Abdoulaye allows himself a smile on seeing me. What must the chauffeur and he think of our duet behind their mask of respect? The servants were the Mandingo marabout's prime worry. Not Mabo Julie who was part of the family. The others. Deep down, I'm his true daughter.

This will have been the first night that Ibrahima Sory has spent entirely with me except at Samiana where he could hardly do otherwise. Which proves that political upheavals in a country have their advantages and strange consequences. I have not the heart to try and laugh. At three o'clock in the morning I'm dead with fatigue, fear and shame. To stop myself uttering the unfortunate name of Saliou, I had to start over and over again. Transform any questions I might let slip into moans or sighs. All this noise of lovemaking is to get rid of my conscience. I ought to say consciences, both of them. The one you always get rid of when making love. And the other. I managed very badly. At the most unexpected moments the gates of the camp would open and Saliou would appear limping wretchedly along an unending road, then lost round a bend. Sometimes the gates wouldn't open. So I climbed up and discovered naked, mutilated male bodies in an amphitheater. I had to turn each one over to find Saliou. Then I found him under the amphi seats, smiling, but considerably thinner. His wound was bleeding in the middle of his forehead. Oh, let's sleep. At Heremakhonon you can't hear the muezzin's first call.

I would never have believed that Oumou Hawa would take refuge in her own family. But there she is on the other side of the hedge at Ramatoulaye's.

"They'll have to release him since they haven't got proof."

I can remember Yehogul one day at the dispensary saying you can make up proof. And I'm inclined to believe him. That's how she keeps her convictions. Yesterday she waited four hours outside the office of the head of police who admitted her in the end, consoled her and advised her to see Mwalimwana. She is getting ready to go to the President's palace. What about Ibrahima Sory? Perhaps I'm naive, but wouldn't he be the first person to contact? As they say in their proverbs: blood is thicker than water. Well? She shakes her head.

"I don't want to disturb him."

Disturb him? What does that mean?

"If I ask him something he doesn't want to do, I'm disturbing him."

This code of behavior is completely beyond me. At least Ramatoulaye's point of view has the merit of being clear. When you have a husband who has lost his job, who has been arrested twice in thirty-six hours, who leaves you without a cent and obliges you to take refuge at an older sister's (fortunately with more money), then you leave him. At her age and with her looks, Oumou Hawa will have no trouble finding another husband. Oumou Hawa shakes her head. Not in outright indignation. But as if she is rejecting an idea she doesn't share. As I said it's not like them to be demonstrative. So I was afraid of Oumou Hawa setting eyes on me. She showed no surprise on seeing me at Heremakhonon. None of the contempt I had feared. Perhaps she's afraid of disturbing me too. Ramatoulaye sighs.

"How is all this going to end?"

You might very well ask. The radio nevertheless has resumed its normal programs. It needed all this to get me to listen to the radio in this country. I listen as I imagine millions of anxious others listen for news of relatives. It seems that only the town has been shaken by this bout of fever. An announcer, who reads his report very badly, takes the opportunity of praising "the citizens of the regions" whom the West has not tainted. What has the West got to do with it? No need to add more crimes to those it has already committed. Then I jump, as he announces that Ibrahima Sory has been appointed President of a Public Welfare Committee in charge of judging all subversive élements as soon as they have been brought out of hiding. He then launches into praise of the courageous Minister for the Defense and the Interior, first recalling the nobility and seniority of his family and interrupting to let a "griotte" sing in a high-pitched, harmoniously discordant voice about a certain Koli, a more or less mythical ancestor of this illustrious family, Abdoulaye explains standing next to me. Now I understand. Ibrahima Sory is the dauphin, the man on the rise. What a hecatomb in view! It'll be like everywhere else. All the agitators will be liquidated. Personal hatreds revenged. As well as rivalries and disillusioned ambition. And when you think that Ibrahima Sory is to orchestrate all that! Because that's what he is going to do. If I think too much about it I'll go back to town. Basically, are the events in this country any more sickening than reading my daily about incidents in Latin America, Hungary or Iran? Couldn't I not care a damn? Couldn't it simply be a topic of conversation back in Paris?

"You were there during the trouble? Do tell us about it . . . "

You start to recount, embellish on the two shots you vaguely heard. For the traveller in modern Africa, the coups and other uprisings have replaced the elephant tusks, the lions and the tigers. It would be like that if Saliou—a friend—were not in danger. Perhaps what I'm witnessing in such a fragmentary and imperfect way, like Fabrice on his battlefield, is the fight of a people for their liberty and justice. But I am moved because a friend is in danger. Am I to be pitied because I have no idea of the major sentiments? I only know the minor ones—friendship, love. My ancestors, my ancestors via Ibrahima Sory are playing a dirty trick on me. A very dirty trick. By imprisoning Saliou they are trying to force me to hate them. Ramatoulaye is right to ask where all this is going to end.

Agossou has me admire some enormous mauve dahlias that have just bloomed. His hand is the color of soil. His nails are all broken and chipped like old crockery. Shall I cry on his shoulder? Tears have never changed anything. The garden overlooks the sea which you reach by a goat path. Ibrahima Sory's brothers are climbing it and shouting gaily. They don't care a damn either. They are children, the privileged few. They greet me politely as they go by. If I try and go down there, I'll break my ankle. The sea down below is lashing the rocks.

Perhaps I'd better go back to town. Pierre-Gilles would keep me company and tell me how his love life is progressing. If worst comes to worst, we could go and have a pastis at Jean Lefevre and Adama's. Jean Lefevre will tell us about Rouen. Yes, my ancestors are playing a dirty trick on me. They are laying a trap. They are making me choose between the past and the present. Take sides in this country's drama. As if they too are fed up with my objectivity. What am I going to do? I can stare at the sun and the sky through the leaves of the flame trees until I fall into a kind of torpor the way I used to when I was a child at Herone. Usually when I was a bit sad without knowing why. A very dirty trick.

Has Oumou Hawa come back from the President's palace? They say Mwalimwana adores pretty women. What's the betting he's going to offer that age-old bargain: you sleep with me and I'll free your husband. A bargain that a loving wife accepts in good grace. I've had enough. What if I packed up and went? Jean-Michel was flippant at the airport:

"When you've found your ancestors, you'll come back to us, I hope?"

A pack of ancestors who are torturing me, that's what I've found. Well, don't let us dramatize. Let's keep as confident as Oumou Hawa who has gone to knock on another door. Ramatoulaye is seeing out a man who looks preoccupied and greets me without a look. As he goes off in his red sports Mercedes (what a shocking color on such a day), she takes me by the arm and tells me he is a rich businessman, highly esteemed by Mwalimwana and formerly engaged to Oumou Hawa who still loves him although she had to get married. Which is normal at her age.

"Oumou Hawa has always been stubborn. She would have been happy with that man."

No, I can't stand it anymore. I have to go into town. I'll come back, I'll come back, Abdoulaye. I have to give myself the illusion of doing something, you understand.

It's awful how quickly things return to normal. The town is still swarming with soldiers and police, but has almost resumed its normal routine. The heat of the alert is over and everybody has gone back to their little patch of misery. The shops are open again. The beggars are chanting. The children are buying peanuts and fighting. The taxi driver whistles.

Pierre-Gilles tells me not to go on appearances. The repression is awful. Over two thousand people have been arrested. Some of them have been piled into an open stadium a few miles from the town as the prisons are overflowing. Where does he get his information from? Still my wretched objectivity. He makes a wide gesture.

"That's what they say . . . "

They can say anything. He looks at me with a critical eye.

"You look terrible. That man, darling, isn't doing you any good."

That is an understatement. A game of bridge? Why not. With whom? Not Jean Lefevre and Adama whom he doesn't especially like, having the same opinion of them as Saliou. A colonial and a whore. I'm the only one who can stomach them. A game of bridge? No, perhaps not, after all.

Pierre-Gilles may be right, perhaps the prisons are full. But life has gone back to normal. Why? Indifference towards those who got caught? Or fear of being suspect in turn? Life is like a mushroom that spreads over any terrain. Over the rich black humus, along the mossy trunk of old trees, under dead rotting leaves.

Abdourahmane's children are jumping up and down on my bed. Not at all repentent, they rush into my arms. Children are fond of me. Aida and Jalla are always surprised that my nephews who only see me during their parent's holidays in France think of me, send clumsily colored drawings and photos. Let me listen to the radio.

The announcer whom I've grown to detest without ever seeing him, simply from the sound of his voice and because he speaks too fast, swallowing certain words, reducing others to pulp except for the t's and r's, announces that the Public Welfare Committee (I haven't the strength to laugh at this name) held its first meeting late into the night (that I know as Ibrahima Sory turned up around two in the morning when I had given him up) and decided to set up a people's court to judge the leaders of the revolt, the brains that dragged in their wake millions of mystified individuals to whom Mwalimwana in his goodness will grant forgiveness as soon as they have made amends in public and sworn to walk straight along the path of the revolution. Let us not have any illusions! They're not going to free Saliou either tomorrow or after tomorrow as Oumou Hawa hopes. They'll judge him for his brains, and the militants, fearing for their lives, will shout guilty out of sheer terror.

And he'll get fifteen or twenty years in prison. Perhaps ten with a bit of luck. And if he behaves well, they'll let him out at the end of seven, thinner, older, limping miserably as I saw him in my dream, along that unending road until he comes to a bend. When he comes out of prison, I shall be far away! I shall be far away, that's for sure. But where? Does that mean I can't escape them anymore? They'll be at the airport. All around me, trying to forget the past. Yes, yes, she did do one or two silly things when she was young. Who didn't? Now she's back. We've kept Dr. Ferdinand Surinam, a confirmed bachelor so he says, in reserve for her. Yes, yes they'll have children, and like us they'll prove to those disbelieving whites that the bourgeoisie can be black, perfumed and classical music-minded. Calm down my friends. Do you know what's going on in your country? Fifteen or twenty years. Enough to become an old body, as they say where I come from, blinded by the sun. What has Saliou done to deserve that? I shall never know. It's impossible for me to search for the truth. You don't become an investigator overnight.

Even so, we have to live. What is Oumou Hawa going to do? Probably hope, hope against all the odds. What do all these prisoners' wives do? I don't know. I have never met any of them. You see them in the films—carrying knives to cut the bars, hidden in loaves of bread. Well, we have to live. Let's get stoned drunk to start with. With our colonial and our whore.

No, I'm not going to get drunk. A young boy around fifteen whose face seems vaguely familiar is in the living room.

"Papa asks you to come and see him."

Papa? He explains: he is one of Yehogul's countless children. Some people have a taste for detective stories, spy novels and other similar works. Not me. I once started a detective story on a train between Paris and Honfleur. I never finished it. With fate mocking me I follow the child several feet behind—so that we don't look as though we are together, he tells me, delighting in the situation, given his age and despite the real tension. I hesitate in front of Yehogul's house and check that no soldiers are following, ready to grab me by the neck.

"There you are, thank you for coming."

Could I have refused?

"Friends have warned me. They've signed my arrest warrant. They'll arrive at any moment to take us to the airport."

His wife is dressing the children. A shy, little woman to whom I have never had much to say during our rare meetings. Through the window, the street looks quiet and sunny. On the pavement opposite, a modest stall with roasted peanuts, pimentoes and okra.

"You must do everything possible to see Saliou. That won't be difficult for you, will it?"

This question hits me more than a reproach.

"Tell him he and his friends must not lose hope. We are going to arouse international opinion."

Oh, please, don't make me laugh. International opinion doesn't care a damn. One nigger more or one less. Perhaps you think that the television stations in Europe and America are going to interrupt their programs? That you'll make the headlines? I can already see you relegated to page four, just good enough to illustrate the chaos-that-set-in-after-the-whites-left.

"Tell him, tell him."

Yes, I'll tell him. If I manage to see him. That won't be as easy as he thinks. I'll tell him because he'll need hope to put up with his four walls. Do you think he's in there for long?

"Twenty years. Not less! They're too frightened . . . "

Twenty years. He'll really be an old body.

"Don't cry. You women, you like crying too much. Tell him . . . "

Yes, I'll tell him. Even if I don't believe one word of what I say.

"If I were you, Veronica, I'd keep out of all this."

Pierre-Gilles is right in a way. In his opinion, my visit to Yehogul was highly imprudent. Not that he's insensitive or indifferent. But reasonable. I've never been very reasonable, fortunately. Yes, I'll talk to Ibrahima Sory. It'll be yet another laisser-passer. If only the time would go faster and the sun would leave its zenith where it reigns like an idle king. He can't refuse me that. What are the prison cells like? You hear so many things. They say they are sometimes no higher than four feet and the prisoner has to live crouched in his stinking excrement. Let's think of something else. Of what? What can you think of at a time like this? Reading seems drab and insipid. Any music seems shocking. Perhaps they torture, too. They put electrodes on the testicles. Prison, torture, these are things you never dream of having to think about. And what if Ibrahima Sory refuses? He won't. What if I went to Heremakhonon to keep my impatience at bay? Abdourahmane is sleeping in a hammock in the garden that he has hooked up to a tree. He's got it easy. A boss who is absent half the time and never passes a finger over the furniture. His second wife who was spitting blood is better. It seems it wasn't tuberculosis. Something to do with the stomach. She's pregnant. A bit early nevertheless to go to Heremakhonon. It will only make a change of scene, not make the waiting any more bearable. Perhaps a ride into town?

The soldiers have virtually disappeared, although there are still a lot of police. Passers-by, especially children, are in front of the Party's National Headquarters whose walls have remained intact, but blackened by the fire. A barrier of militia with their tricolor belts, one of them is seated behind a table writing. People are lining up for some reason. A man tells me: "It's for the card."

Always pieces of information that never fit together. How many of these men and women care about Saliou? How many know who he is? I'm sure these students do. But the citizens from the regions? Those from the North, the fief of Ibrahima Sory? From the dense, impenetrable forest with trees over ninety feet high, so they tell me, where the villages are lost in a torrent of green? That too has to be discovered. It's terribly important. But how? Can I run from one to the other asking do you know Saliou? If they do, they'll be afraid to admit it and will shake their head. If they don't, it will pain me enormously. I pass by the Alcatraz. Kadidiatou, the little prostitute, is perched on her bar stool. Yes, life is back to normal. Two others, vulgarly made up, thick lips, smiles. Kadidiatou leads me to the other end of the bar.

"Baké's been looking for you."

So what? What does she think of all this? She motions to me to keep quiet and I follow her eye to the cashier who is sitting idly behind his till yawning, disclosing a very bad set of teeth. We empty our glasses, beer and grapefruit juice, respectively. Why don't I come to the Miami Club anymore? And my husband, the white man? And Amar? Oh, Amar! She has no idea. A quiet place to talk? She casts another glance at the cashier. Yes, she'll come to my house . . . At the Plaza they're showing *The Rider from Arizona.* A woman is lying on a cloth with her triplets between her knees. The taxi driver is convinced he knows me.

"You've forgotten! I haven't."

What does he think of the recent troubles? He looks at me in his mirror and I feel that his answer will depend on what he sees.

"Mwalimwana did the right thing! Too much riff-raff, too many hooligans!"

What did I expect? I pay. I'd need to be somebody else to make this investigation. To start again from the very beginning. To emerge again from my mother's womb. Not in the vast mahogany bed with Mme Aristide, the midwife, wiping me with a soft toweling, slipping me into a very fine linen dress embroidered by Mlle Euripide, the best embroideress in town, and predicting that I'll be the very portrait of my father, and she's seen some births in her time, before opening the door to the Mandingo marabout, disappointed at having another daughter, but glad it's over. Perhaps on the ground in a hut brought forth by Cherubine who, despite the starting pains, finished her day's work tying sugar cane because money is hard to come by and you can't count on your man who runs after younger things and doesn't worry about all those hungry mouths to feed. From the very beginning. Now it's too late. It's too late, isn't it, Abdoulaye? Some manage to start again. Do they? Well, they'll have to let me in on the secret.

Everything is too late. I'm not going to start moaning now. Abdoulaye is crouching beside me once again, one hand holding the silver teapot with the conical lid, the other the little cup made in China. Did he know Saliou? Why ask all these questions? He goes off. His baggy trousers rubbing together with a soft sound as he walks.

And what if Ibrahima Sory doesn't return tonight as is sometimes the case? Or too late and harassed, going straight to his room, disturbing nobody but Abdoulaye? No, no. God wouldn't allow it. God?

Once when I was sixteen, I was standing on the balcony and I said, squeezing my eyes tightly shut: "If God exists, make Jean-Marie go by on his motor bike." I opened my eyes and there he was. He didn't give me a straight look as the Mandingo marabout was standing beside me exchanging a few polite words with Mme Reynalda. I was struck by it and, at the same time, fell into my own trap, as I didn't want to believe in God with all those believers around me, but here was proof, wasn't it? I have to go home. How shall I broach the question? Well, I'll plunge right in without bothering about diplomacy. Why should he grant me a favor he refused Saliou's own wife? Oumou Hawa spends her time in vain going from the President's palace to the Ministry. She is received everywhere with apparent cordiality, but does not obtain the authorization she seeks. Why not?

I have to see Saliou. Not only to give him Yehogul's message. For him to explain. I'm illogical, absurd. All the time I was with him I refused to listen. I reproached him for wanting to influence me. For painting a bleak picture. For inventing things even. Or else boring me. You have to admit he didn't exactly make you laugh. Why doesn't Ibrahima Sory come back? The sun decides to move. Without hurrying. It's going to take hours to cross the sky. To descend to meet the sea which will gradually lose its deep rich color like a washed out indigo cloth that borders on blue. Hours.

I wait on the terrace. I wait in the little salon where the

horsemen from Burundi merely aggravate matters with the raucous sound of their horns and the hooves of their horses. I wait in the room where Abdoulaye has placed Agossou's mauve dahlias. What shall I ask Saliou when I see him? If he is guilty of the crimes he is accused of? And if they really are crimes or a counterattack in an attempt to put an end to them? Whether his violence is in response to another, more underhand and secret, that has become a daily occurrence carried out with impunity under the guise of Law and Order.

Mustn't fall asleep. You always fall asleep. And then I'm back on the terrace as if I'd only dreamed I'd left it, but I know I did because the sun which was in the middle of the sky is now starting its monotonous descent. Well, I'll go and look for Ibrahima Sory at the Ministry or the prefabricated building that houses the Public Welfare Committee at the corner of the avenues M. Gandhi and Patrice Lumumba. Abdoulaye advises me to stay quietly here as he's bound to come back, change and rest a little. What a life these events are steering him toward! There we are, both of us, and not knowing what to do I turn the knobs of the radio as it will soon be time for the news. I have become an ardent listener, reproaching myself for the childish dislike of this announcer whom I have never seen. I'm right, he's just started reading, stumbling over his words as usual. Abdoulaye and I listen and we hear him announce that Saliou, the former director of the National Institute, who had been arrested a few days earlier has, out of remorse for his crimes widely attested to and of his fear of facing the people's court, taken his life by hanging himself from the bars of his prison cell with his trousers. At that very moment (life has its coincidences that outdo the most melodramatic novels), Ibrahima Sory enters, worn out. He goes straight to the radio, turns it off by pushing the first black, square button with his forefinger, turns around and says:

"It's better that way."

What do I expect?

Oumou Hawa has her head covered and is sobbing between two women I've never seen before whose eyes are brimming with tears. Ramatoulaye too seems shaken sitting in the salon with a large number of other visitors. The grief is not for Saliou. It's for the widow and her suffering. And everyone here present in their sadness still accuses Saliou as though having predicted how it would all end. He should never have fallen in love nor brought children into this world. A few mourners are wailing in the compound. It's the custom to call them in out of respect for Oumou Hawa so that it is not said that her husband did not leave her without a penny and the family didn't do the right thing.

They'll go home soon. What do I expect?

Oumou Hawa's baby is asleep hanging on the back of Hafsa who is mending a hem and shouting to the children to be quiet. They have been put into her care, but are fighting under the lemon tree. Over the hedge I can see Agossou leaning over his rose buds. The sweat is streaming down his face and to check it he has tied a dirty rag around his forehead. He is whistling between his teeth.

I have seen death twice. The first time was my grandmother who filled a room with her coughing fits, her potions and quirks. The second was Mabo Julie. And each time I was shocked by how little someone you thought essential mattered. A few days after the death of grandma some workmen came and transformed her gloomy room that smelled of turpentine, tea and another very special smell, into a sort of light, airy boudoir where my mother used to sit with friends. They would look through mail order catalogs from the Paris shops and have us recite our lessons. As for Mabo Julie! Ah, Mabo Julie! Since Aida, Jalla and myself were big enough to wash and dress ourselves, we hired just a cook. Literally. A young, impersonal woman who had worked for the Bakra, proof that she was clean, honest and knew her job. When I looked in through the kitchen window, which was now out of bounds, I saw that she had taken down Mabo Julie's

Baby Cadum and replaced it with a Coca Cola ad. On it was a blond American smiling under an enormous red and blue capsule, astride a bottle. She had also installed an electric clock, not content with the old, round unreliable one which Mabo Julie swore she was the only one who could make work. She asked for the white, half-broken high chair where Mabo Julie used to put me when she was concocting one of her delicate sauces to be taken away. She didn't like dirt cluttering up *her* kitchen. One day I was watching this abomination from the garden and the Mandingo marabout, who was passing by, saw me. He guessed what I must be feeling and as, let's be honest, he wasn't inhuman, he pinched me gently on the cheek.

"Well, what do you expect."

Yes, what did I expect?

"It's better that way."

What does that mean, in your opinion? Either it was better for the rat to kill himself because we are going to do him over. Impossible. I don't believe it. Saliou wasn't a coward. Or else, and my intuition tells me this must be the truth, they killed him and chose to camouflage his death by suicide. They thus dealt him a double blow, depriving him the martyr's crown by cancelling his option to become a model prisoner, glorified by reclusion. And giving a warning, a brutal warning to his admiring fanatics. So they went to all that trouble which means it was worth it. He had a following, an importance I never suspected, blinded as I was by the mediocrity of his mode of living and his insignificant personality. They can't tell me I haven't any proof. I have stacks of it. You *can* make up proof. I feel it. Therefore I know.

And now what's going to happen? Will the town react to being crushed by the recent violence, by all this show of force? No, the town is fed up, too. Nobody will say a word! Tomorrow the body will be returned, it seems. They'll bury it discreetly. Anyway, Moslem funerals are not spectacular. Not the least bit? I don't believe it.

The announcer has repeated the message five times already. Something is going to happen. The President's palace or the Matanko mosque or the central police station will go up in flames. A man, a woman or an adolescent will stop in the middle of the street and scream: NO! Perhaps some are sobbing. Where? Behind closed doors so that the prowling soldiers don't hear them. Can you blame them? What am I doing? Standing in the shade of the flame tree. Looking at Agossou. I hear the children shout and their arguing voices. I haven't fled Heremakhonon. Simply because I don't have the strength. Literally. The sun. The sun. And what if I were mistaken? What if the town, the whole country changed into a flow of lava and the men from the land took their hoes and tore off the branches from the trees? Obviously, I'd like to see a general slaughter. To prove they had miscalculated. Oh, how they had miscalculated! And that this death is not of little significance, benign and meaningless. In any case, isn't death always meaningless? The poor sods who are told to go to the front are led to believe otherwise and bang! They're given a medal posthumously which is a fat lot of good to their children. Saliou won't have a medal. I want to die. Baloney. Nobody wants to die before his time. What about those who commit suicide? You won't commit suicide. He didn't commit suicide. How do I know, after all? I know. Besides, the story doesn't hold water. It's now a classic. It's already been worn thin by East and West alike. One of the children pulls me by the hand. He wants me to take sides against Thierno who has just pinched him hard. Where is Thierno? In the lemon tree, his little white teeth in a wide grin.

What do I expect?

Let's wait for the night! By day the sun is a super cop from whom nothing is secret. But the night is persistent. Thick. The formidable depths of the African night were felt by travellers, explorers, traders and missionaries alike. Perhaps it will generate courage. Perhaps it will generate strength. If they come out, I'll join them. I've hesitated too long. I've played my little doubting Thomas. I wanted proof, proof. Enough talk. I'll join them. I've lost too much time.

Pierre-Gilles has just bought me a book. Jean Lefevre and Adama some illustrated magazines. Jean Lefevre, biting on his short-stem pipe, repeats for the tenth, perhaps the hundredth time:

"In my opinion, it's sheer madness. An expatriate's contract is worth a gold mine. And you're throwing it all over."

Pierre-Gilles understands me. Not that he'd do the same if he were in my place. But he understands the reaction, he told me. That you'd blow everything sky high. He's wrong. On the contrary, I'm trying in my fashion, the only way I can, to save something. There's a crowd of people around us. Not many travellers, as it's not easy to leave the country. I mean officials. Except for foreigners who only have to surrender their resident's permit to the Ministry of Foreign Affairs and pay their ticket—in foreign currency. Idlers fascinated by the DC-10's and Caravelles or simply dreaming. Pierre-Gilles is sad. He says he'll be terribly bored when I'm gone. I'll leave some regrets behind after all. Abdourahmane's wives cried a lot. Fodé, Sidiki and the other children, seeing them cry, started up too. It was touching. Now stop pretending. I was moved to tears. But I have to go.

Nothing happened. I watched the sky in vain. Listened. Nothing. The town slept, like a drunkard with a fetid breath. The plane has been delayed an hour. Which means killing two long hours in this brand new airport, built to the glory of Mwalimwana. Mwalimwana the builder.

Oh, let me get out of here! Let me shake the dust of this country off my feet!

"Like a pastis?"

No, I don't want a drink. I want to leave with my head clear. Fully conscious of what I'm doing. It's nothing rash. It's not a spur-of-the-moment decision. I've understood. *Understood.* I must leave if I want to maintain a semblance of respect. Because there is a level below which one must not go.

"You'll write, won't you? You must write."

If only the plane would arrive and we could get it over with. If only there were fewer people milling around. Why are they so agitated? Buying magazines or rather leafing through them without buying. Which annoys the salesgirl. Admiring the flowers. Where do they come from? Probably from the national nursery at Samakon. Another feather in Mwalimwana's cap. Be careful, it's easy to ridicule. It's because I'm tired of waiting. Waiting for this plane. Heads all turn in one direction. As during a game of tennis. A woman has just entered the hall. Her gold lamé boubou floating behind her. Her Charles Jourdan shoes clicking elegantly: Ramatoulaye, princess of Belborg. We embrace. She was a good sort after all, however much she gossiped. She is holding an oblong-shaped packet in her hand.

"An embroidered cloth, the way you like them."

Well, I'll have something to show after all. Together with the mask Pierre-Gilles gave me. And the little copper statuettes from Jean Lefevre and Adama. What will I do with all these exotic things? I abhor exoticism. And Oumou Hawa? Oumou Hawa left for the North with her baby. The North where I'll never go. After such an ordeal she needs a mother's attention and the affection of the old father whose favorite she always was. Saliou's older brother is taking care of the eldest children. That's normal. He's a primary school teacher at Tenigbé. Not at all a hothead like his brother. Who had everything to make him happy. Well, let's not blame the dead. Yes, the dead. Already dead a long time. I can see what's going to happen. I saw it from the very start. In six months, a year at the most, Oumou Hawa will give in to the repeated pressure from her family. And will marry again. To her faithful suitor or another. Who would throw the first stone? She's only twenty-six. Ramatoulaye insists that I write. She'll write. She often has things to order from Paris that you can't find here—padded bras, perfume and hair lotion. And I'll have to buy all that for her? Yes, yes. She might accompany her husband on one of his missions. So we'll see each other again. Oh yes. She embraces me. I return the kiss. An hour's delay is too much. She goes off.

"A lovely lady she is."

That's Jean Lefevre commenting.

"Yes, the Northerners are good-looking. But they're barbarians!"

That's Adama who is from the forest and jealous of Jean Lefevre's comment.

The town slept. With clenched fists. I soaked my pillows in tears. If you think about it, I've cried a lot during by brief stay in this country. Fortunately in seven hours I shall be far away. Far away. And time will lose this sluggish pace that is driving me batty. It will get faster and faster amid the din of the metro, the chaos of the traffic jams and the rush hour. Oh quick! Deliver me up! Telepathy! I look round. The glass doors of the airport open and in comes Ibrahima Sory. He's dressed in one of his Mao suits which he keeps to now as he must have been advised that his ceremonial boubous make him appear too royal-blooded to be the savior of the Revolution, President of the Public Welfare Committee and member of a newly-created tri-partite presidential commission responsible for assisting Mwalimwana.

The crowd recognizes him. Which isn't surprising since he is always on the front page of the *Quotidien Unique.* The soldiers and police, here to keep order, stand to attention. He motions to them very slightly which is meant to dismiss them as well as to salute the crowd to acknowledge its recognition of him. He is secretly practicing for the day when Mwalimwana will have been devoured by wolves much like himself. They are still trusted for the time being, but he will outsmart them all.

He comes up. He gives a little arrogant salute to Pierre-Gilles, Jean Lefevre and Adama which neatly signals them to clear off. They understand perfectly well since they move away and pretend to admire in turn the flowers of the national nursery. He hands me a heavy, square object wrapped in a soberly elegant paper. What a lot of presents I shall have received after all. I thank him. He puts his hands in his tunic pockets.

"Abdoulaye can't get over your leaving."

Abdoulaye? Yes, Abdoulaye. And what about you?

Say something, my nigger with ancestors. You know, don't you, why I'm leaving? I'm leaving because it would be too easy to stay. If I stayed, nothing would change between us. I'd continue to shuttle back and forth between Heremakhonon and the town. Until one of us got tired, you the first, of course. In a way nonetheless despicable and cruel, although bloodless, I've helped to kill him. Finish him. So that nothing remains of him. *Nothing.*

I am convinced that if that night the town hadn't slept, if men, women and youngsters had come out of their huts, I would certainly have marched with them. Their determination would have given me strength. Is that what would have happened? I shall never know because they remained behind closed doors, lying on their lice-infested straw beds. And here I am. Face to face with myself. Trapped. For ever. For ever? All this time he's talking. What's he saying?

"It's Spring now in Paris."

Spring? The streetcleaner on the Rue de l'Université will have taken off his thick, blue turtleneck sweater that shows under his overalls. Will he have noticed my absence? How will he welcome me back? Yet another flight! One day I'll have to break the silence. I'll have to explain. What? This mistake, this tragic mistake I couldn't help making, being what I am. My ancestors led me on. What more can I say? I looked for myself in the wrong place. In the arms of an assassin. Come now, don't use big words. Always dramatizing.

Spring? Yes, it's Spring in Paris.

The End

Maryse Condé was born in Pointe-à-Pitre, Guadeloupe in 1937 and after local schooling through the lycée classique she took university degrees in Paris and London. Her career has embraced radio and television, journalism, teaching (in Europe and Africa), and she is an active reviewer and critic. Her creative work has been in several genres (drama and short and long fiction) and she has edited one francophone collection of literature (Ghana, 1966).

Heremakhonon (Welcome House) is Maryse Condé's first novel (Paris, 1976) and this is the first translation of any of her work. Her newest novel **Une Saison à Rihata** appeared in Paris in 1981.

Her play **Le Morne de Massabielle** was performed in 1970 (Théâtre-des-Hauts de Seine de Puteaux) and later dramatic works **Dieu nous l'a donné** (Paris, 1972) and **Mort d'Oluwemi d'Ajumako** (Paris, 1973) have been published. Three Continents Press will publish English translations of both in 1984.

Heremakhonon means in Mande (Mandingo) "Welcome House." Certainly for Veronica, the self-exiled Antillean heroine of this novel, there was a very special welcome. In Heremakhonon there was power, modest beauty and luxury, and even a steely kind of love. But in and outside of Heremakhonon—at her school, in the country, on the streets of the capital—there were also invitations to learn that violence, and ambition often cloak themselves in the same words, gestures, and importunities, as idealism, self-sacrifice, and virtue.

Told in a mosaic of feelings (from childhood and adolescence in Guadeloupe, from her university days in Paris, and her increasingly dubious experiences in Africa) this novel is a tract, a self-analysis, and a cry! Self-denigrating, never pitying, the words of *Welcome House* invite us to forego our easy pieties to enter the acrid world of modern Africa—a world the Africans did not make but which somehow they must endure and survive.